Not Quite
ᴬSpinster

Not Quite A Spinster

REBECCA CONNOLLY

second paperback edition
April 2023

ISBN 978-1-952103-55-1
Library of Congress Control Number 2023904677

Acknowledgements

For Kitty, who has been so patiently waiting her turn. I hope you find this worth it!

And for York Peppermint Patties. A true friend in times of need.

Want to hear about future releases and upcoming events for Rebecca Connolly?

Sign up for the monthly Wit and Whimsy at:

www.rebeccaconnolly.com

Chapter One
London, 1820

———— ⧼∽⧽ ————

There is nothing so maddening as the beginning of a courtship. Uncertainty, awkwardness, stilted conversations, competition with others vying for the same individual… Quite a flurry of emotions, all things considered, and it is enough to terrify any sensible creature out of the venture. If there were any sensible creatures in Society, of course. Which, we all know, there are not.

-The Spinster Chronicles, 11 August 1818

Lieutenant Edward Henshaw was tired of waiting.

Patience might have been a virtue, but it was certainly a nuisance, particularly where a young lady was concerned. He had been close to pining for one particular young lady for over a year, and the feelings were only growing more intense by the day.

Which would not have been a problem had she been aware of the attraction. But she was not.

He was a coward.

No, that was not fair. He was not a coward; never had been. He was an army man and had served his country faithfully. He was considering retiring his commission, but one could never be certain the world would not require a good military man to assist in settling unrest in the coming days and weeks.

He would have found such a calling upon his duty far simpler than his present task.

At long last, he had decided that he was done with waiting for the perfect opportunity to present itself. He was going to behave with intention toward the young lady of his particular interest.

Miss Catherine "Kitty" Morton. Younger sister of one of his best friends. Shy creature of unbelievable extremes, proficient in a great many accomplishments, and the most beautiful woman he had ever seen in his entire life. Utterly perfect in complexion, fair with a natural rosiness in her cheeks that had tempted his fingers incalculable times, dark sable hair that he would have paid his entire fortune to see unbound, and a smile that had the ability to completely remove his spine from his body.

He had spent the last year and a half, give or take, working to become a man she could feel comfortable with, someone she could trust, someone she could smile in the presence of, someone who would not frighten her merely by appearing. He could do nothing about his towering stature or the broadness of his shoulders, the gruffness of his voice, the fact that he could appear more animal than gentleman purely on his appearance, but he could do something about his manner and his behavior.

And so he had, to the point where, unfortunately, he was barely noticed by her. She was so comfortable with him that her brilliant blue eyes skimmed over him like they might have done words on a boring newssheet. Her smile was only for him if he had been especially amusing in a way that had garnered her notice. Their conversations were nothing monumental and did not even warrant further consideration once removed from the occasion. Not only was she completely at ease in his company, she did not even blink when he entered the room, as he so often had done.

From would-be suitor to a panel of unremarkable wallpaper.

He had strayed too far.

But so tentative had he been in taking this further step for fear of ruining something between himself and his best friend—as well as the tenuous fibers of trust between himself and Kitty—that he had balked at his own wishes. Kept them completely to himself so that no one might suspect. Told himself that time would be enough, and somehow what he wished for would miraculously come about.

Then his friends had wound up finding marvelous brides for themselves, and his other acquaintances had married in turn, leaving pretty much only himself and the heiress Charlotte Wright without matrimonial partners.

Some might have suspected that they would marry each other, but they were rather more like bickering siblings than would-be lovers and would not have suited at all. If either of them sought love matches. Which, as it happened, they both did.

Charlotte was a member of a rather notorious group called the Spinsters, capital S required, who spread about a newssheet on their own called *The Spinster Chronicles* that was quite popular. Despite all of her fellow Spinsters relinquishing the lowercase version of their title, she had yet to do so.

Only a few weeks ago, Edward had sat in a drawing room with Charlotte, listened to her bemoan being left out of the matrimonial bliss her friends had found, and somehow found himself wagering with the woman on who would marry first between them.

A hundred pounds and the name of his or her firstborn child were at stake.

Why in the world would he do something so unutterably stupid?

Confidence had coursed through him at the time, knowing how reluctant Charlotte had been, and was, about seriously pursuing romantic relationships, but now he had become aware that she was, in fact, quite determined now.

Which meant he had to be.

How could he pursue Kitty on the heels of a wager? The entire idea was disrespectful to her, and yet he had done so as though he could win the woman in any five minutes given him.

Idiot, idiot, idiot.

He was far more likely to fail on doing a perfect recitation of Shakespeare's most romantic sonnets, purely because of the boredom his performance would incur. Was it more difficult to win the affections of a woman he did not know at all, or one he knew so well that she could not be bothered to care when he came to call?

He would never suspect or accuse Kitty of being callous or cold where he was concerned. She was not capable of such dark, haughty feelings. She simply had grown so accustomed to his presence that it had lost its luster. She was as kind as ever, as warm and charming, without pretense or fanfare and without the defenses she had once had in the presence of any person unrelated to her.

He would never regret that portion of their association. Could not. She was more beautiful beneath those carefully constructed layers than she was in appearance, and he had not imagined such a thing possible.

As he had grown more in awe of her, she had grown more comfortable with him, both of which seemed to make their romantic possibilities more far-fetched.

And he had wagered on it.

He had gone directly to the Mortons' home to speak with Sebastian and his wife, Izzy, on the subject, feeling quite sure that he could not pursue Kitty in earnest without her brother's consent. Izzy, being a rather good creature and a nice one besides, had offered to leave, but Edward had insisted she remain as well. Not only to ensure that Sebastian did not rise in a fury at him but because he suspected she might have more influence on Kitty than Sebastian, and he needed her as an ally.

Surprisingly, the meeting had gone very well, and Sebastian had given his consent for Edward to attempt a courtship and take it up in earnest if Kitty wished. The complete lack of resistance to the idea gave rise to several questions on Edward's part, but he had walked away without asking them.

He suspected his feelings were rather more obvious than he'd previously thought, which was oddly unnerving.

In a desperate attempt to begin his efforts and improve this situation, and partly to rid himself of the stain of wagering on something as permanent as marriage, he'd decided to go to the theater this evening, knowing that Kitty would be in attendance with Sebastian and Izzy. He'd not specifically informed them that he would also attend, but once they saw him, as he intended to present himself in their vicinity, he would be invited to share the box with them.

Knowing Sebastian Morton's proclivity to hold his wife's hand at any moment possible, he would expect them to sit beside each other, leaving a seat free beside Kitty. As she was so comfortable with his presence now, it would raise no suspicions or questions. He could only hope that some bored gossip would catch sight of it and suspect something between them. In London's rather rumor-hungry circles, such a tale would require some careful interventions, and he would happily sacrifice himself to a marriage with Kitty to preserve her reputation.

It would hardly be so neat and tidy, and Kitty would never survive the mortification of those rumors, so it would be a doomed sort of marriage that would shame him for the rest of his life. A poor substitute for what he dreamed, and a cheap imitation of what Kitty deserved.

Which meant he needed to behave with caution and care, just as he had been doing for the last year and a half with Kitty. But also with precision. Which he had not done.

He had created a mess for himself, and he had never thought pursuing a marriage prospect would be so difficult. The oldest of his seven sisters had managed marriage without any trouble at all, yet here he was, whimpering in a corner about the whole thing.

Some soldier he was.

Perhaps he ought to resign his commission after all. He was clearly not worthy of it.

All the London theaters were destined to be crowded and congested with patrons on any given evening during the Season, and tonight was no exception. It was a dreadful crush, to use a phrase, and Edward did his best to push through without actually shoving any person aside.

It was enough to be wearing his regimentals rather than standard eveningwear, which was destined to make him stand out more, but to be actively seeking out certain persons while attracting attention was the absolute worst. He could have worn the alternative, he supposed, but as he did not know what else he might stuff his person into for such an occasion, his uniform had seemed best.

First step forward, and he was already failing. Not exactly the encouragement he was looking for.

The interested expressions of young ladies who only sought out the finery of regimentals met his eyes everywhere he looked and only heightened his anxieties about his present situation. There was nothing a marriage-hungry miss and her equally determined mama loved so much as a man actively in pursuit of the same, even if she were not the object of his affections. Failure to secure an engagement once tried was the perfect opportunity for such a young lady to present herself as a pleasant alternative, no shame at being second choice anywhere to be seen. It was a voracious world of underhanded behavior that frankly ought to have been frowned upon rather than celebrated, but that was indeed the way of it.

He hated every second.

He could only hope his attempts to secure something with Kitty would not be so blatant as to catch the notice of anyone else. The last thing he needed was to be prevented from spending every possible moment with her because of a blockage in his path. She would never see him as her own candidate if there were others in the way. She did not think highly enough of herself for that.

If Edward had his way, she'd have been the envy of all women in every circle, in every nation in the world. She would hate such attention, but he would shower it, anyway.

Modesty was becoming, but not to the extremes of doubting the validity of praise. She must learn to value herself, at least a little, and see herself as being worthy of attention. She would never extend so far as to expect any such thing, but surely she could learn to accept it without demurrals.

It was the only flaw he could possibly find in her.

He was intelligent enough to know that she could not actually be as perfect as he thought, but he was pleased to let himself be so deluded.

Edward sighed as yet another young lady attempted to slow his progress by placing herself just enough in his path that he would have to maneuver around her. A more gentlemanly man might have excused himself and made polite conversation, creating an opening she would immediately seize. But he did not. He kept his eyes focused ahead of him and made the adjustments in his movements to continue on without difficulty, not even glancing back to check her disappointment. Such an action would only encourage whoever she was, and there was only one woman he was in any way interested in encouraging.

And she did not even see him.

Yet.

Good heavens, had the Mortons changed their minds about coming to the theater after all? This was intolerable, wandering through crowds that held absolutely no interest for him. He was not feeling particularly unpleasant toward any of them; he simply did not wish to be generally social.

He had no time for that. He needed to be specifically social, and that was that.

"Henshaw!"

He bit back a groan at a feminine voice calling out to him, wondering when young ladies, or their mothers, had grown so bold as to call out after a man in a public place. But then, on reflection, that voice belonged to a particular woman who had no daughters to marry off and whose company would be a fine alternative if he failed to find the Mortons.

He turned slightly to his right, seeking the source, then smiled when she broke through the nearest group of people. "Good evening, Miranda."

Miranda Sterling, stepmother to his good friend and former fellow soldier, Captain Anthony Sterling, was the most interfering woman he had ever met, the most outspoken, and generally the most entertaining person, male or female, of his acquaintance. He utterly adored her at least three quarters of the time.

The other quarter he wished she would find a better occupation for her time than whatever she was fixated on.

She looked rather elegant, as always, her still mostly dark hair pulled back into rather intricate styling, her gown that of rich green silks, and her eyes bright with the light of the theater corridors. And her smile was not at all mischievous, which could either be promising or terrifying.

"Good evening, Henshaw," she returned with a regal nod. "I did not know you favored opera."

He shrugged his shoulders, grinning. "Favored is a strong word. I don't mind it, to be sure, and when in the right company, it can be rather good."

Her eyes narrowed, informing him that his word choice had been rather poor. "And whose company is right this evening?"

"Who else?" he hedged, still grinning. "The Mortons. Izzy is

7

forever trying to culture me, and my sisters have yet to receive permission from my mother to come to London and try it out. I must prepare myself for the day she gives in to their pleas, should it come."

"Let it never be said that I doubt a brother's devotion to his younger sisters," Miranda said at once, her expression clearing, though something in her eyes still not quite convincing him. "And Isabella will certainly instruct you as to the finer points of opera. Kitty, however, is the music lover. Perhaps she might guide you as to the more emotional side of things."

Edward bowed a little, keeping his smile in place. "An excellent thought. But would you not advise me yourself? I know full well you are musically gifted and musically educated, so why not join us?"

"Dear Henshaw, do you think I can abandon my friends and plans just to help you comprehend the details of *La Cenerentola* on a whim?" Miranda shook her head, huffing an irritated sigh that did not fool him for a moment. "Ridiculous. Whatever would I tell them?"

"That all depends," Edward replied easily. "Do you like these friends, or not?"

Miranda's eyes flicked to him. "I adore them."

"Then you would be all apologies if I could persuade you away. But you need not. Just know that, in the future, if your friends were barely tolerable, you may use my ignorance as an excuse for yourself." He bowed as though he could declare himself her servant, and her laughter was the only thing that brought him upright once more.

"Oh, you are a good sort," she praised, patting his arm. "I simply must set my mind to finding a wife for you one of these days; after I've finished with the Spinsters, of course."

That was an interesting caveat to the offer. "Oh?" Edward asked with mild curiosity. "You're nearly there, it's only Charlotte left."

"And Kitty," Miranda added as she snapped open her fan. "I know she is not technically one of them, nor is she a spinster of the lowercase variety, but I count her one of their little band, so she will also receive me as a benefactress in that regard."

"How fortunate for her," Edward murmured, his stomach twinging in discomfort at the idea. "Would you like me to warn Morton now, or—?"

He was soundly rapped on the arm by a fan. "Say nothing, or

you will ruin it all," she insisted. "Besides, Charlotte will require more attention, so it may be some time. Now, go and find the Mortons before the overture. It will give Isabella time enough to prepare you." She gave him a warning look and swept away with all the grace and pomp with which she had arrived.

He shook his head after her, just as bewildered and bemused as he was every time he encountered the woman. And he had no problem with doing just as she said, though it would not be to find Izzy, that was quite certain.

He moved down the elegant, red papered walls of the corridor without much interruption from anyone else, which was a blessed relief. Just when he thought he was going to have to go completely around to the far side of the theater from his present position to find them, he caught a glimpse of striking copper hair and turned toward it.

As he'd hoped, such hair belonged to Izzy Morton, standing arm in arm with her husband, and she grinned warmly at his approach. "Lieutenant Henshaw! Have you come to enjoy the opera this evening?"

He gestured in a playfully grand manner, returning her smile. "I have indeed, and in the hopes that you might have an open seat in your box so that I might not be left entirely on my own for the duration."

Sebastian raised a brow, smiling slightly. "Doubting your ability to behave without supervision, are you?"

Edward gave his friend a sour look. "I daresay I would be appropriately composed, but I would do better with the watchful eye of your wife to keep me in check. Surely even you can agree to that."

"For you? Certainly, I can."

"Sebastian!" a new voice scolded on a laugh. "Are you suggesting that Izzy does not have an equally calming influence on you?"

Edward's chest clenched as his eyes slid past Izzy to the radiant person of Kitty Morton, arrayed in a gown that near-perfectly captured the color of her eyes, dark hair curled and twisted with simple elegance, and a band of jeweled flowers stretching across the darkness like a tiara fit for the loveliest of princesses.

And she was smiling, heaven help him.

The sudden vanishing of his spine sent fire down both legs and clenched his hands into fists. "Miss Morton, my apologies," he said with a quick bow, his voice not quite steady. "I did not see you there."

"Oh, I don't mind," Kitty said at once, waving the apology off. "No doubt you saw Izzy's beautiful hair and knew exactly where to go. I look like a dozen other girls here tonight, and Sebastian like every other man."

The statement was not true, but it would do no good to contradict her.

Thankfully Izzy broke in before he had to answer. "Sebastian is better under my influence," she informed them all with a quick smile. "He never smiled like this before."

Sebastian's smile was for her alone, and that was clear as he looked at her with all the adoration in the world. "I never had a reason to smile like this before, my love. Can you blame me?"

"Oh, that's lovely," Kitty said on a laugh, looking between her brother and his wife with a fondness that belied the attempt at sarcasm. "He's only had me for my entire life." She sighed and looked at Henshaw playfully. "Would you sit by me this evening so I might not feel so abandoned by my brother, who apparently has never smiled because of me?"

Catching the game in a single stroke and desperately trying to ignore the ocean of relief sending wave after wave over him, Edward nodded with an utter fervency none of them would believe if they knew its depth. "I will, Miss Morton, and I assure you, all I will do is smile for it." He offered her his arm, completely turning his back on the other two, which made them laugh.

"That would be most welcome," Kitty answered, slipping her gloved hand through his arm and lifting her chin a little, which made her delicate blue earbobs dance.

As though this entire scheme had been his plan all along, Edward led her into the box in full formal procession, not even bothering to hold the curtain open for Sebastian and Izzy behind them.

"Have I shocked them?" Kitty whispered, still laughing as he led her to a chair. "It isn't like me to employ sarcasm, but I have been spending some time with Charlotte."

Edward groaned playfully. "Oh, Miss Morton, don't say it—"

Kitty giggled. "You like her, Henshaw! You've said as much regularly. And you can call me Kitty, you know. We are, after all, friends."

He knew that. He had known that. But to do so now, knowing what he intended…

"In your home, certainly," he told her, not quite laughing now. "In the home of our friends, yes. But here in public? I daresay it would be better if I did not."

She smiled at him, igniting the space where his spine had once been. "Suit yourself, but know that I give you permission."

He would cling to that until the day he died, no matter how any of this turned out.

Edward cleared his throat, eager to move back to a safer conversation. "And yes, I do like Miss Wright. But it does not follow that you should become like her. The world has Charlotte Wright already, so I insist you remain Kitty Morton."

"What's this?" Sebastian asked as they came behind them. "Kitty wants to be Charlotte?"

Kitty rolled her eyes, which was also a very Charlotte thing to do. "No, I simply said that my attempts at sarcasm are due to her influence, and that is all."

"Heaven help us," Sebastian muttered, shaking his head. "Don't tell her that. She'll think she's won something."

"I think Charlotte is a little busy at the moment for small victories," Izzy assured her husband with a warm pat to his arm. "Finding a husband and all that."

"I still cannot believe that," Kitty said in a hushed tone. "Why now?"

Izzy smiled at her sister-in-law softly. "She feels left out. I don't think it is the right reason to start, but there is no convincing her otherwise."

Kitty frowned at that. "I thought she wanted to marry for love and nothing less."

"She now believes she can will herself to love whomever she chooses," Izzy replied. "Time will tell, I suppose."

The music of the overture began before they could get Kitty's thoughts on that score, which was a trifle disappointing to Edward.

11

He wanted to know any and all thoughts she might have on love in general, no matter how the subject came about.

They sat in their designated chairs, Edward taking the one beside Kitty, just as he'd hoped, and, once settled, turned to Kitty to continue a quiet conversation. Only to find that she was completely transfixed by the music and focused on the stage, despite the lack of actors at the present. He did not exist at the moment.

That was all right, he supposed. He could talk with her at other times in the show when her awe and fascination faded. He would look for every moment possible and take advantage of it.

He had to.

Chapter Two

$\mathcal{A}$ shy girl is the most difficult one to manage, and one must occasionally venture most creatively to bring about desired results.

-The Spinster Chronicles, 6 September 1816

Kitty Morton sighed as she left the home of Charlotte Wright, where the most recent meeting of the Spinsters had been. It had been as entertaining as she had hoped it would be, and twice as rewarding. The Spinsters had taken her in when she had first arrived in London, given her brother's natural reserve and indifference to much of what Society had to offer. Izzy had gone on to marry Sebastian, of course, but the others had become quite good friends to Kitty and had given her introductions to other young ladies with whom she had also become great friends.

Given she did not meet the age requirement to technically be a spinster, in the lowercase sense, she was not officially one in the uppercase sense either, even though she had written for their *Spinster Chronicles* a few times. Elinor Sterling, formerly Elinor Asheley, had not been of an age either, but her sister had been one of the original members of the Spinsters, so they made allowances for her. Kitty didn't mind that in the least; she enjoyed enough of an association with them to keep her quite content and had given her enough distance to avoid the unfair stigma Society had given the group.

Occasionally, Kitty went to their meetings, more for the chance to socialize with them and hear what would be in the next issue of the *Chronicles* than anything else. Today, she had been able to discuss her exquisite evening at the opera a few days prior. *La Cenerentola* had been a stunning experience, undoubtedly destined to become her favorite of the Rossini operas. The story of Cinderella had been a favorite of Kitty's for many years, but to see it played out on a stage with such skilled musicality was simply sublime.

She had been unable to look away from the stage the entire evening, which made her rather poor company for her brother, Izzy, and Lieutenant Henshaw. She doubted any of them were so devoted to opera as she was, so she hoped they had found a way to enjoy themselves while she had been so wholly distracted. She had conversed a little with Henshaw during the intermission about their favorite numbers from the first act, and then again at the end of the show about their feelings on the pieces in general, but it had been clear, even to her, that he was being polite in the conversation.

He had not been miserable, she knew that as well, but he was no opera lover. It was sweet that he had tried to be encouraging and share in her delight of the evening, but he would need to attend several more operas or study music a little to really converse as she longed to. Izzy indulged her some on the carriage ride home and at least knew music well enough to understand what she was attempting to say, but Sebastian hadn't been entirely content with being wholly left out of a conversation in their presence.

What she would not give to have shared the experience with Alice Sterling. She was a great music lover as well, and while she was a trifle more outspoken than Kitty, she would have been well matched in energy on this particular topic.

Alice had a lovely singing voice and had no fears in sharing it. Kitty could not sing if there were any other people in hearing range at all, and, given the closeness of quarters in their London house, that was a constant due to the servants. She was even terrified of them hearing her. She had only just grown brave enough to allow her brother to hear her play, though he was not permitted to be in the room when she did so. Izzy was permitted, but only because she could correct Kitty if need be and help her when necessary.

Kitty could be a passionate admirer and advocate of music, but never a performer in it. Never.

And that was not something she regretted, really. If she ever felt brave enough, she might do so, but if not, music would be her quiet love in life.

She did not need to be on display to enjoy music.

"Kitty, wait a moment."

Kitty turned in surprise, the voice not belonging to her sister-in-law, who was only a few paces behind her. This voice belonged to Izzy's cousin and best friend, Georgiana Sterling, who had been with them at the meeting of the Spinsters, and who rather felt like an older sister to Kitty, much as Izzy did.

Georgie smiled warmly as she approached, her bright green eyes made more lovely by the morning light. She was still in the process of tying her bonnet ribbons, batting away a stray blonde curl that had gotten tangled in the fabric. "Thank you. I had hoped to catch you before we left the drawing room, but Charlotte kept me longer to ask my opinion on Mr. Riley, for whatever reason, though I don't know him from anyone."

Kitty snickered softly. "Is she very interested in him, then?"

"I think she'd like to be, if he meets her approval in certain areas, but who knows?" Georgie shrugged a little. "I came to ask if you might come home with me just now. Miranda is coming and asked me to bring you along for tea. Iz, please come as well. You may play nursemaid to the lot of us, though I doubt Kitty will be the one who requires it."

"I shall do my best," Izzy replied with a laugh. "Kitty?"

Kitty could only stare at Georgie in shock and with quite a bit of apprehension. "What does Miranda want?"

Miranda Sterling was Georgie's husband's stepmother, and she was terrifying. Wonderful, but terrifying. Interfering and terrifying. Determined and terrifying.

Utterly terrifying.

She had once commandeered Kitty for company on a carriage ride, just after Kitty had arrived in London, and interrogated her the entire drive to the modiste. But then she had paid for the entirety of Kitty's gowns and acted as her benefactress for the rest of the Season. She was generous and warm, had a wicked sense of humor, and often inserted herself into the lives of others for matchmaking purposes.

What exactly she wanted with Kitty now was quite mysterious, which was all the more... well, terrifying.

"I haven't the faintest idea," Georgie admitted with a sigh that told Kitty she quite understood the melee in her mind. "I only know she cannot stay long, as she must attend to particular business with someone's valet or tailor, though what gentleman should be so descended upon I could not imagine. I know it isn't Tony."

What gentleman's tailor or valet Miranda may or may not have been meeting with after this tea was of no concern to Kitty, unless it meant the interlude involving her would be restricted to only five minutes of time.

She would be quite interested in keeping things short.

There was no refusing Miranda, for whatever reason, so Kitty found herself nodding and biting back a sigh. "Yes, of course."

Georgie smiled. "You are a dear. Don't worry, I'll keep her from too much mischief. She's rather preoccupied with Charlotte's mess at the present, so I doubt it can be so very bad."

If only she sounded convincing in saying so.

Still, it was not as though Miranda was a villain. Everything she did was with good intentions, even if she went about it in a rather bold way.

Anything bold made Kitty chafe, whether she was the one to do it or not.

They walked together to the Sterlings' home, the distance of a few blocks doing a world of good for Kitty's nerves, as well as her stamina. Growing up away from the fuss of London at the family home near Bedford, Kitty had grown used to frequent walks in the relative countryside and getting some fresh air and exercise on every fair day available to her. In London, things were a trifle different, and even walks in Hyde Park could not entirely compensate.

She had reveled in returning to Lindley Hall for the autumn and winter, the comfort there a blessed relief from the tumult London thrived on. The winter had been mild enough, so she had been fortunate enough to walk often, and she had done so.

Whomever she married, if she married, would do well to have a country estate with paths she could walk at her leisure.

She was not destined for London life, no matter how amusing portions of it could be. A quiet country girl was Kitty Morton, and so she wished to remain.

Miranda was waiting for them at Georgie's house, seated by a small table in the parlor, where a tea service had already been set out.

"Good day, my dears. I hope you do not mind that I have begun without you. At my age, and with my vast demands, one must take advantage of every moment's respite."

Georgie and Izzy laughed while Kitty merely smiled a little. "At your age?" Georgie repeated. "A mere number, Miranda, and you are not to be defined by it."

"True," Miranda conceded with a dip of her chin. "I do excel in that regard. Come, sit down. The tea is still hot."

They did so, Kitty feeling a little put out when Georgie and Izzy took the furthest seats from Miranda, leaving her to sit just at her elbow.

This felt more like a battle than a simple tea, but perhaps that was her imagination.

She sat and quickly poured herself some tea, adding just one lump of sugar before stirring quickly and bringing the cup and saucer up.

"Kitty, my dear, I am positive you are curious as to why I asked Georgie to bring you to tea," Miranda said before Kitty could even blow on her tea to cool it, let alone take a single sip.

Kitty took a moment to pause and consider her response. "I was a little confused, I will admit," she finally replied, wishing her voice did not sound so small and timid. "But I was not reluctant, I hope."

"You sweet girl." Miranda reached out and patted her knee, her smile a trifle pitying. "Hesitation and reluctance are not the same thing and should not be confused for each other. You are too good to be reluctant to see me, but hesitation is perfectly normal, considering what you have seen of my machinations."

Well, that was a relief, and it softened something that had been pulling at Kitty's chest from the moment the invitation had been offered. She nodded and managed a smile before taking a small sip of her tea.

"And so?" Georgie prodded on Kitty's behalf, which earned her a grateful smile.

Miranda did not so much as flick her eyes in Georgie's direction, keeping the blue-gray gaze locked on Kitty. "I should like to start you on a course of entertaining the attentions of select young men, all personally approved of by myself or the Spinsters, in the hopes that a courtship might blossom from it."

Kitty immediately blushed, her cheeks flaming beyond anything she could recall previously. "What?" she whispered weakly.

Miranda tutted very softly. "Oh, my lamb. I knew you would hate it. But surely you do not wish to remain unmarried forever? And in order to have a marriage of more than politeness and arrangement, you really must do something. This is really a very small something, when you think about it. All will be very gentle, I assure you. No one will descend upon you en masse, and we will not dangle you before bachelors like a prize to be won. Do you believe me?"

She believed nothing and no one at the moment, her throat tightening with the same burning fire raging through her cheeks, rendering her incapable of words.

"Knowing Kitty's particularly shy nature," Izzy prodded in her kindest voice, "how would you suggest this venture proceed in a way that will not be excruciating for her?"

Oh, was that all? To avoid the excruciating? To be uncomfortable every moment so long as she would not die from it?

"I have given that every consideration," Miranda assured Izzy, her voice seeming to come through a fog to Kitty's ears. "We will arrange for a small gathering to be hosted at the home of one of our friends. We might have two or three of our candidates there, but also several friends in whose company no one will feel awkward, especially Kitty. We are not to draw attention to the scheme, as that would be rather distressing for Kitty."

This was rather distressing for Kitty, and still she was having to sit here and endure it. But, rationally speaking, being introduced to two or three young men in the company of friends without being thrust at them was more palatable than something more grand.

She had met several people during her time in London, introduced by a friend every time, and her discomfort at such introductions had faded a great deal since the first. But to have men introduced to her for the express purpose of creating interest...

She would attract the attention of anyone looking, simply by being shockingly flushed at every moment. No one would find a constantly red-faced miss in any way attractive or appealing, so the scheme would be for naught, anyway. Only it would ruin her for any future attempts that she or anyone else might take on to help her marry,

Miranda was right; Kitty did wish to marry. But she wished for it all to transpire naturally and without force. Without effort, if she were to be brutally honest. Something so easy, so comfortable, that mortification would not dare show its face.

Was that so naive and far-fetched an idea? Was she a child for believing such a thing was possible?

"Kitty, you have danced with practical strangers before, have you not?"

The question broke through Kitty's thoughts with shocking clarity, bringing her attention to Miranda dazedly. "Yes," she managed slowly. "Not often, but yes. Alice usually makes me. She knows everybody, so she arranges for dance partners for us both. It seems easier when it happens that way. Less pressure."

Miranda made a sympathetic sound. "I am afraid we must exert a little pressure now. Not much, but some. You deserve to be danced with on your own merits and not your friend's."

It would be lovely to have that be the case, but Kitty did not mind the other way around. Whatever the reason, she was meeting people, gentlemen in particular, and who was to say that one of them would not find Kitty to their liking, her shyness notwithstanding?

Now she was to be the focus, and the idea of any such thing was too much to bear.

She sipped her tea again, this time nearly gulping it down in her desperation to be too occupied in doing so to respond to anything else.

"And have no fear, I will not put you on display."

Wouldn't she, though? Was this not exactly that?

"No playing for company, no singing, no displaying of your art or embroidery. I will not bring particular attention to you in any way."

Ah, that sort of display. Small mercies to be spared there.

Kitty swallowed hard and looked at Miranda, who seemed to see more than Kitty wished. "Please don't think me ungrateful,

Miranda—"

"I don't, darling," Miranda assured her quickly.

"…but why?" Kitty went on, acknowledging her response with a nod. "With Charlotte Wright going on her husband-hunting rampage, why would you bother with insignificant little me?"

Miranda set her tea down and turned more toward Kitty, taking one of her hands. "First of all, Catherine Morton, there is nothing insignificant about you, and if I ever hear you say such a thing ever again, I will cause a very great fuss over you indeed."

Biting back a very small laugh, Kitty nodded.

"Secondly," Miranda continued, "Charlotte needs neither my help nor my intervention. I believe she will find her own way, for good or for ill, and my involvement in her affairs will tend in another quarter entirely, but that is my secret. You, on the other hand, are just the sort of good, sweet creature that may benefit from my encouragement. I aim to see you very happily settled indeed. Not necessarily well settled, you see, but happily. That is my point."

There was a distinct difference between the two, even Kitty could see that, and she felt marginally better about becoming Miranda's project if happiness was the aim. A good marriage meant a great many things to a great many people, and while Sebastian certainly wanted her to be taken care of in her future, Kitty was convinced her happiness was more important than her situation to her brother.

Georgie cleared her throat softly. "Kitty, I will grant you a boon in all of this. If you should ever feel overwhelmed or unbearably uncomfortable, you need only come to me. I will get you away from whatever place we are in and do what I can to recover your evening."

Miranda huffed an impatient sigh and gave Georgie a hard look. "You cannot give her that opening each time, Georgie. I have no trouble with your boon, but kindly limit it."

"Half as many events as you will have," Georgie relented, rolling her eyes. "Is that a fair enough number? Or must I reduce it further and say a third?"

"Three boons," Miranda insisted firmly. "No more. I have told you that I will not parade Kitty about, so you can hardly think more than three will be required."

Georgie gave Kitty a look. "If we have used up our three, kindly go to Camden Vale if he is about. He'll take care of it."

Kitty nodded obediently, smiling at the idea. Prue was one of the Spinsters, and her husband, Cam, was a rascal in the most entertaining way. He was very protective and had fallen in love with Prue despite her own troubles with nerves, shyness, and anxieties. He would perfectly comprehend Kitty's state, should she grow overcome, and would not care two figs for whatever rules Miranda had set up for her.

"Oh, bother with Camden," Miranda muttered, shaking her head but smiling all the same. "A villain after my own heart if there ever was one. Don't distress yourself, Kitty. We will hold a card party at my sister's home next week to start, and it will all be very quiet and comfortable."

There was nothing to do but nod in response, and Miranda rose the moment Kitty did so.

"Off again, Miranda?" Georgie asked with a wry grin. "The tailor and valet of your mysterious gentleman?"

Miranda sniffed dismissively. "Never you mind. You will know my aims by and by. Suffice it to say, it has nothing to do with anyone in this room, nor for my plans for any of you. Breathe easy. My intent is on another person entirely." With a nod, she glided from the room with more poise than Kitty could have managed had she practiced every day from the age of three.

There was silence in the parlor once she had gone.

"Well," Izzy finally said, bringing her tea to her lips and sipping softly, "that was unexpected."

"Mildly," Georgie agreed dryly. "And here I thought she wanted Kitty to write something for the *Chronicles*. She's been asking about it for ages."

"Has she?" Kitty murmured, her fingers feeling cold despite the teacup in her hands. "Does she know which ones I have written in the past?"

"If she has, she has not said so to me." Georgie shook her head, exhaling roughly. "She knows you've written for us, of course, but you know I never say which articles anyone has written in there."

Kitty nodded, not particularly minding if her identity was known among their friends for her columns. She did not flatter herself that she was a gifted writer, but she did enjoy anonymously expressing herself, and her compliments from the Spinsters themselves were lovely. Izzy was the writer in her family, however, and Sebastian her illustrator. Their stories were endearing and, Kitty hoped, would soon be made available to the world.

She looked at Izzy with a little concern. "Will Sebastian mind that Miranda is doing this? I don't want to upset him."

"I don't think so," Izzy replied, which disappointed Kitty just a little. "So long as she takes the care she said she would about it. Your brother would love to see you happily settled in your own marriage and family, but he would never push you. Nor would I."

Kitty knew that, at least. Knew it well. Which was, perhaps, why Miranda had decided upon this course in the first place.

"There is no refusing Miranda, is there?" Kitty inquired of the other two, her earlier statement to herself on the subject now coming into question.

"It's not exactly advisable," Georgie said with marked hesitation, "but it can certainly be done if you wish it."

It was on the tip of Kitty's tongue to say that she did wish it, that she wanted to overthrow the entire plan, no matter how much thought and care had gone into it, and that she wanted to return to Lindley Hall and be done with London forever.

But the words would not come. Refused to be spoken. Vanished from existence.

Did that mean that, in her heart of hearts, she did want to do this? That she did wish to find a husband sooner rather than later? That she was willing to succumb to Miranda's plan in order to do so? That she would place herself directly in embarrassing situations in order to have the chance at a happy marriage?

Where had this come from, and why had it not made itself known before? Where had this bolder side of her been all her life?

Kitty found herself shaking her head. "No, I will do it. Miranda will not embarrass me; I know that much."

"This is true," Izzy agreed calmly. "She would be so distraught if she thought she might."

"A little discomfort, perhaps, but no embarrassment," Georgie added.

"Then I will be well enough," Kitty told them and herself. "I may have small regrets, but no very great ones."

Georgie handed her a plate of biscuits, her smile kind. "Have you any idea of gentlemen you might wish to know better? Any that have caught your eye?"

Kitty shook her head, the heat in her cheeks finally beginning to ebb away. "No, not especially. I have to say, I barely notice. It has not been my aim, you know. I suppose I shall have to look now."

"Sometimes, they find you," Izzy pointed out with a laugh. "Quite unexpectedly."

Recalling how she and Sebastian had been thrown together, Kitty found herself smiling. "Yes, do let me know if any of the gentlemen have a shy sister coming to London that I might help. That would make it all very tidy."

"We will find someone who gives you your very own story, Kitty," Georgie told her rather firmly. "Not some faint imitation of anybody else's. Your heart will know what it wants when it finds it, and all we can do is help it look."

"I suppose that is true," Kitty said softly. "But I've never considered what I might want in a husband, which makes this all seem very daunting indeed."

"Don't think of it as looking for a husband," Izzy suggested. "That could be anyone, depending on the sort of marriage you want. We are looking for a friend for now, and perhaps that friend could become more."

It was an interesting idea, even if it were not entirely true. Yes, they wanted her to be well suited to her husband, and friendliness would be a good start, but in the end, what they wanted was marriage.

She would have to convince herself to pretend otherwise if her sister-in-law's thought was to work.

Could she pretend that far?

"A friend," Kitty repeated, testing the word out to see if it was in any way more comfortable.

It wasn't.

She sighed and tried for a smile. "I'll see what I can manage."

Chapter Three

———⚬∽ ∾⚬———

Small gatherings are far worse than great ones. There are never enough partners for conversation, rarely any good card players, and if no one is skilled at music… It is far better to feign an illness than to ever attend such tepid affairs.

-The Spinster Chronicles, 25 July 1815

It was, without a doubt, the oddest gathering at the Johnstons' home that Edward had ever attended. Miranda Sterling was their hostess, there was no question, but she had not taken her own house in London, choosing, just as she had last Season, to live with her sister and her husband. They indulged her taste of social gatherings, and Mrs. Johnston shared her sister's tastes in many ways, though with a touch more reserve.

At least one of them possessed some.

What was odd about this particular gathering was that there was practically no one there. Perhaps a dozen people, if that. Only half of the Spinsters and their husbands were present, and notably, Charlotte Wright was not one of them. That was not especially surprising, he supposed, given her foray into husband hunting, but she was a staple in all events, so her absence was noticeable.

It was not like Miranda or the Johnstons to limit their numbers so, not when they had space for far more. The sound of the gathering was so low that Edward could have cleared his throat and everyone would have noticed. Surely someone ought to play music to encourage conversation between the guests and to put them all at ease. But Miranda would know that, so why was it not happening?

And why was he so concerned about the oddity of this gathering? He must be growing fussy the longer he spent in London and Society. He'd have to remove to Bristol soon to visit his family and remind himself of his true self, though he could not think of doing any such thing until his primary task at the present was accomplished.

For good or for ill.

He cast a glance around the room, noting the presence of Georgie and Tony Sterling, their cousins Elinor and Hugh Sterling, and Sebastian and Izzy Morton to represent the Spinster contingent. Then there was Peter Rafford, a puppy if there ever was one, Frederick Atkins, the curate who was weak on his best days, and John Brayler, who had just inherited his uncle's title and fortune and had yet to lose his bewildered expression for it.

Bachelors all three, and not exactly part of Miranda's usual circles.

Amelia Andrews and her husband were present, which would make for good conversation, and then there was Kitty Morton, seated at a card table that housed Miranda, Rafford, and Brayler for a round of something or other.

His thoughts slowed as he took in that particular table.

The only unmarried woman in the room, apart from Miranda, was Kitty.

Three bachelors and Kitty.

Well, four, if he counted himself, but he was not certain he was meant to count in that regard.

Oh heavens, what fresh madness had he stepped into tonight?

Sebastian saw him and whispered something to Izzy, then came over to him, bearing the expression Edward might have worn for an event like this on one of his sisters' behalf, should tonight be what he thought it was.

"Hensh."

Edward nodded once and gestured toward the card table. "Is this what I think it is?"

"An attempt to get Kitty admirers without anyone else's influence?" Sebastian suggested in a dry tone. "Yes, exactly. Miranda sprang it on Izzy and Kitty at tea the other day, and nothing I could say or do would shift it."

"With Miranda at the head, that is not surprising," Edward mumbled, shaking his head. "So, no Charlotte, no Alice Sterling, no one else who could possibly take attention away from her? And no music?"

"Because of dancing, apparently." Sebastian shrugged. "They don't want it."

Edward snorted softly. "Who is going to suggest dancing when we all know good and well why we are here and that dancing is not wanted? Honestly, get Mrs. Andrews to play something so this isn't so awkward."

"But Kitty—"

"Kitty would feel more comfortable with the music to fill the silence, I can promise you that," Edward overrode with as much firmness as he dared.

Sebastian gave him an assessing look. "You do realize such a knowledge of my sister's tastes ought to have come from me, do you not?"

"If you paid half as much attention to your sister as I have in the last eighteen months, you'd have been able to," Edward told him without shame, smiling a little to soften the blow. "But your heart was captured by a very lovely woman, so there is nothing to regret."

"Speaking of hearts being captured…"

Edward gave him a look. "Will you put my name in Miranda's hat? She would take it up like that bloodhound of hers and never let go. Neither Kitty nor I would react well to that."

Sebastian held up his hands in a gesture of surrender. "Fair enough. Just know that I'd prefer you to any of those three Miranda scraped up."

"If you were your sister, that would mean a great deal." Edward gave him a bland smile and gestured for him to move toward the Andrewses. "Music. Please."

Sebastian nodded, chuckling about something or other and did as he was bid. Amelia brightened at the request and moved to the card table to ask Miranda's consent, which was given, although there seemed to be conditions on the thing.

Likely no songs that could be danced to.

A pity, that. Edward could have used the excuse to take Kitty from what had to be a deuced awkward situation and at least make her smile.

If he could offer her nothing else, he could promise to make her smile.

If only that could be enough.

The music soon began, soft pieces without the energy that might bring about dancing, and it seemed as though the entire room breathed a sigh of relief with the change in the sound about them.

Edward grunted in satisfaction at that. He might not know much about music, as the miserable failure at the opera could prove, but he did know when it was needed.

He moved across the room to the bowl of punch, filling a cup for himself and turning to survey the room again. Tony Sterling met his eyes and nudged his head in a clear beckoning. With nothing better to do, Edward joined the circle with both sets of Sterlings present.

"Anyone for another table of cards?" he suggested without much enthusiasm.

No one in the group took up the idea.

"They're almost done anyway," Elinor murmured with a faint gesture at the table. "Rafford has been more interested in Miranda than Kitty."

"Oh my days," Tony groaned, looking heavenward. "What is it called when someone marries your stepmother?"

"Your stepmother," Hugh assured his cousin, "would never marry a puppy. In fact, I don't think she'll marry again at all. If I know her, she'll be quite disgusted that one of her candidates has missed the mark and he'll be scrubbed from the list."

"Good riddance," Edward muttered, taking a quick drink of punch. "And Brayler?"

Georgie made a considering motion with her head. "He seems to be managing his own. He's polite enough to talk with Kitty, so we must give him credit there. And she seems to be managing her blush fairly well."

"Is such a thing actually managed?" Edward wondered aloud. "No doubt this was supposed to be a comfortable gathering."

Nods bobbed around. "I think it is too small," Elinor chimed in with a wince. "I'll say as much to Miranda when I have a chance."

"I wish you well, my dear," Hugh told his wife somberly. "My step-aunt does not enjoy being corrected or advised."

Elinor gave him a dark look. "If you think I do not know how to manage conversation with Miranda by now, Hugh, you are sadly mistaken."

He seemed mildly surprised by that and looked around the group. "I'm actually rather encouraged by that. I think I've married rather well, don't you?"

Edward ignored that and looked over at the table, where Miranda laid down her hand of cards with grand flourish, collecting applause from the others there.

"I am quite parched," he heard Miranda announce. "Mr. Rafford, would you fetch me some punch, please?"

He scurried from his chair so eagerly, it was comical.

"Miranda sees full well what Rafford is about," he chuckled. "He's done."

"Then I'll move to the table and take his place," Tony offered. "Georgie? Care to give Kitty a reprieve?"

Georgie looked at him with a question. "What about Brayler? He's still there."

Tony grinned. "And if he's interested, his attention will follow her. Come on."

Georgie blinked, then laughed as she glanced around the group. "I'm beginning to think he learned more from Miranda than anyone ever knew."

Tony pulled her away before any of them could make a reply.

Edward watched carefully as they reached the card table and he smiled to himself when Kitty rose with a grateful nod, excusing herself to get some punch as well.

Rafford passed her without a glance on his way to deliver the drink to Miranda.

Idiot.

Brayler, however…

He watched Kitty go, making no move to leave the table, his expression rather blank. Then he looked at the cards being dealt and did not look up toward Kitty again.

Another idiot, but perhaps less of one.

If Atkins were the least idiotic of the bunch, he would take advantage of the situation. Edward glanced toward the man, currently in conversation with Mr. Andrews, not paying attention to anything around him.

Potentially an idiot, and the only reason he was not an absolute one was that Mr. Andrews truly was an interesting fellow, and he could not blame the younger man for taking advantage of a chance to converse with him.

Though how he could pay attention to anything when Kitty was in the room certainly hinted at idiocy.

If all the intended bachelors were going to ignore the only eligible girl in the room, it only remained for Edward to step in and salvage something of the evening on behalf of bachelors everywhere. The fact that he had little desire to converse with anyone except for the only eligible girl in the room was beside the point.

And it was also exactly and entirely the point.

He turned to see where Kitty had gone and found her standing by the punch table, quietly sipping her punch without looking at anyone or anything in particular. She did not appear to be distressed nor overwhelmed, but neither did she appear particularly pleased.

Interesting.

At as leisurely a pace as he could manage, Edward moved in that direction, plastering a fond smile on his face. It took Kitty a moment to notice his approach, but she blinked and looked up at him as he neared. Her smile was brighter than he had seen in some time, and he felt that she was truly relieved to see him.

Relief was not love, but he'd take it.

"I didn't know you were here, Henshaw," Kitty greeted warmly, lighting corners of his chest he did not know existed with a new fire. "You should have played cards with us."

If only he could have done so.

He shrugged a little, his smile perfectly easy and without effort. "When I arrived, the table was full. I asked both sets of Sterlings if they wanted to play, and they did not seem interested in setting up another table."

Kitty hummed softly and looked over at the pianoforte. "I am so glad Amelia started playing. The silence just stretched on and on."

Edward grinned against the surge of satisfaction that rose within him. But there was no need to tell her the brilliance was his idea. "Was the conversation at cards lacking?"

"Not at all, if Miranda and I are the ones meant to carry it," Kitty replied without shame. "Mr. Rafford gawked at Miranda and stammered a few times, and Mr. Brayler answers questions when asked and occasionally would ask one in return, but it hardly took effort. I am supposed to be the shy and retreating one, but I am coming off as almost sociable."

Her honesty was perfection just as much as it was amusing. "You're rather sociable with me," he pointed out with a laugh.

Her dubious look had him chortling. "I am as shy as shy can be, Henshaw. Just because you no longer bring that out in me does not mean it is not there." She exhaled roughly, shaking her head. "If this is Miranda's idea of entertaining the attention of certain gentlemen, I am in for a very long stretch of things."

Edward sobered a little as he stared at her. "Is that what she's doing?"

Kitty nodded once. "She says that I need a little pressure toward courtship and the like, as waiting for such a thing to happen upon me isn't reasonable. That isn't what she said, I'm adding my own impression of the idea."

Waiting for… Oh, blast. If she only knew!

"So, she's forcing you to receive men of her choice?" he asked awkwardly, trying to restore some semblance of his sanity.

"Forcing is a trifle harsh," Kitty admitted, taking a quick sip of punch, "but it was her idea. She said she would do things gently and not allow me to be swarmed, but this is not what I had in mind. I did not want to be so singled out. As though Mr. Brayler would wish to talk with Amelia all evening, delightful as she is. Or Izzy, much as I adore her. In only inviting married women, myself aside, I've become the most beneficial person for any bachelor to speak with, and I don't like that one bit."

"Don't you?"

She shook her head, swallowing visibly. "I don't want to be

chosen by default, you see."

"No," he murmured, the very idea a ludicrous one. "No, you ought to be the first choice."

That earned him a smile that made his entire spine tingle ominously. "Thank you."

"That's not flattery, Kitty," he assured her. "I mean it."

"I know," she replied, solidifying her position as the most perfect woman in existence. "That is why I thank you. You're not a flatterer, you are just generally good, and I admire that."

Admiration was not love, but he would take it.

"I don't think my sisters would consider me good," he replied to cover his exhilaration. "Not a single one of the seven."

"Oh, siblings are different," Kitty dismissed, waving her hand. "Sebastian would say whatever he thought would build my spirits up, true or not. Or tease me just to see me smile."

"A brother's place is both to irk and protect his sister, I'm afraid," Edward told her with a long-suffering sigh.

Kitty gave him an impish grin. "And which of your sisters do you irk the most, Henshaw?"

He had to think about that, running through each of his sisters in turn. "Probably Thea. She's the third of the sisters and pushes back on any kind of authority. Quite a temper, that one. But also the most mischievous. Easy to nettle, and it is not like me to let an opportunity pass."

His answer made Kitty laugh, the sound musical and filled with the warmth of the sun. "No, I should say not. Did you have many antics between the eight of you at home?"

"Oh, yes," he said with a sage nod. "It is a miracle we all survived to adulthood, and that my parents still tolerate our presence."

"It sounds lovely and mad at the same time." Kitty exhaled a slightly sad sound. "I would have loved more siblings. Not that Sebastian is in any way lacking. In fact, I rather think I am quite fortunate with him as my brother. But he was away so much when he was old enough, and there is such a gap between our ages… It would have been nice to have someone else at home with me."

Edward could have sworn something began to crack deep within his chest. "Were you very lonely?"

"At times," she acknowledged, "but I grew comfortable in my own company and more uncomfortable in the company of others. I suppose that is where my shyness comes from. I don't think I was a bold child, but I don't believe I was quite so timid either."

He nodded in thought. "Our lives shape us in ways we don't notice at the time, but we are changed forever. For what it is worth, I don't think your shyness is in any way a hindrance. It is simply part of who you are, and anybody who wishes to know you better should be brave enough to try."

She brightened immediately, her smile beaming with the glories of the dawn. "Truly?"

The fact that she doubted any such thing made him want to sweep her in his arms to assure her of it, take her face in his hands and kiss her until doubts vanished, or a dozen other dramatic and sincere actions beyond words. But he couldn't do any of them. Not yet. Perhaps not ever, but certainly not yet.

He swallowed with surprising difficulty. "Truly, Kitty Morton. And I defy anyone else who says differently."

Kitty made a soft sound of almost surprised satisfaction and looked out at the gathering, still smiling in a way he would never forget. "How is it that none of those bachelors can talk to me as you do? This is the most comfortable I have been all evening, and where I feel most myself. I do not have to force anything or pretend with you."

He could explain in great depth why that was the case, but he did not think she would prefer that. But it did provide an intriguing thought that he could not entirely ignore, and he began to slowly smile.

He sipped his punch quickly, relieving his dry throat. "I may have an idea, Kitty."

"Oh?" She looked up at him with bemused interest. "For what?"

"This madness Miranda is putting on for you," he said with a faint gesture toward the ringleader currently trouncing the other cardplayers in a game. "Something to ensure that, no matter what the event is or who is in attendance, you have a chance at comfort."

"What's that?"

"Me." He looked down at her with a quick grin. "I'll come to everything. Chances are, I'll be invited as it is, but if not, send me a note. Everybody knows how we know each other, so no one will suspect a thing. Then you can have a comfortable option at any given time, and I can keep an eye on you. Save you from a particularly poor dancer or interrupt tedious conversation—"

Kitty's laughter interrupted him, and he laughed himself at hearing it.

"...signal you to ensure you always win at cards," he went on, warming even more to the game he'd begun, his mind spinning on ever more ridiculous ideas. "Have my carriage at the ready to sneak you away from dreadful events. Create imagined emergencies for anyone with whom you wish to have removed from your presence."

"Oh, stop!" Kitty begged through merry giggles. "Hensh, please!"

She'd never called him by the nickname their friends had, and while it was not exactly calling him Edward, he'd take this as encouragement.

"What do you think?" he asked her, chuckling a little. "Shall I be your own personal social servant?"

"I'd call it a social ally rather than servant," Kitty suggested, laughter lingering in her smile. "I don't want you to wait on me, for heaven's sake. What would you gain from such an experience?"

More than she could possibly know.

"Oh, I'd find something heroic in it somewhere, I have no doubt," Edward said with practiced nonchalance. "But mostly, I'd know you weren't fodder for Miranda's schemes, and that's enough for me."

Kitty stared at him for a moment, then nodded. "All right, I agree. It would be so much nicer to be certain of at least one thing in the chaos Miranda has planned for me. I think I would breathe easier knowing you would be there."

That would make one of them.

"Then it will be my honor to be there to set your mind at ease," Edward told her, unable to do anything about the low, rumbling, hopefully gentle tone of his voice as he said so. "If for no other reason than to make sure you smile."

He hadn't meant to add that part of his wish to the statement, and his tongue burned with the desire to pull each of the words back. Not because he did not mean them, but because of how badly he did mean them and how terrifying it was to have them out on the air.

Kitty cocked her head up at him, her smile a trifle lopsided, which could not have been more adorable. "I think I will smile, Hensh. Seeing you there, I think, will make me smile."

If he hadn't loved her before, he would have then. Sweeping her into his arms seemed like a much better idea, but he could not afford to startle her when she was so sweetly encouraging him to do exactly what he wanted to do—what he needed to do—in order to try for her in truth.

But what else could he do, then?

Smiling back, feeling like his heart might burst into a shower of light destined to ignite his toes, Edward raised his punch glass toward her in a sort of salute.

As if she needed to emphasize her perfection further, Kitty raised her own glass and clinked it with his, her smile still in place.

Chapter Four

———————⁘————————

No one is ready for the Marriage Mart once they are forced to enter it. No one at all.

-*The Spinster Chronicles, 23 November 1817*

"Why am I more terrified now than I was before my very first ball in London?"

"Because you were not actively seeking courtship then?"

Kitty laughed once, the sound sharp and harsh. "I am not actively seeking now, but I'm being made to look for it."

"That's it, we're not going." Sebastian thumped the ceiling of the carriage. "Turn around."

The driver obeyed instantly, shifting the carriage as the horses turned.

"No!" Izzy and Kitty said at once.

Sebastian looked between the two of them as though they had lost their minds. "Are you serious? She's miserable, Iz! Why would I take her into this?"

"I can answer for myself!" Kitty snapped with a slap to the seat of the carriage.

Her brother stared at her in near horror, no doubt startled to see any kind of temper from Kitty.

She nearly apologized but decided against it, shaking her head. "I am not miserable, I am nervous. There is a difference. Hesitation, not reluctance. My insecurities should not dictate what I experience, and Miranda Sterling is offering me a chance to step outside of those insecurities. I might not have sought this out, but if it helps me to find love and a husband, I'll do it."

Silence reigned in the carriage, and still the horses were taking them in the wrong direction.

"Do you even want to get married?" Sebastian asked her softly, genuine concern in his face. "I'll take care of you the rest of your life, so please don't use that as an excuse. You've never said anything about love, marriage, courtship… Do you want this?"

That was the question Kitty had been asking herself for several days now and likely longer, though without any real intensity or enthusiasm. But when Miranda had brought this up, insisting upon it, and forced Kitty to confront the issue…

There were so many questions, and very few answers yet. "Yet" being the key word.

"I don't know yet," Kitty told him, shrugging slightly, "but I'd like to find out."

Izzy's smile was gentle and proud, but she said nothing, content to let the siblings have this discussion without her intervention.

She was so good at giving them that, just as she was about everything else with their lives.

"Very well," Sebastian eventually relented, thumping the ceiling again. "Sorry, Keyes, we're going to the Edens' ball after all."

"Aye, sir," the driver called back. The carriage moved again with the turning motion, rocking them all a little as it did so.

Kitty smiled at her brother. "Thank you, Sebastian."

He nodded almost gruffly. "Just trying to protect you. That's all."

"I know," Kitty replied fondly. "But you cannot protect me from everything."

"Much to my dismay," he grumbled, shaking his head and looking out of the window.

Kitty grinned at Izzy, who returned it as she took her husband's hand. That would settle Sebastian more than anything else. Izzy always had a way of settling him. And she had no doubt that, should they have children in the hopefully near future, Izzy would settle them with just as much ease.

A shaky inhale took over Kitty's lungs, and she glanced out of the carriage window at the night sky and darkened passing scenery as she let the breath fill what it could of her lungs. She slowly exhaled as silently as she could manage. Her brother did not need another reason to doubt their excursion.

Nerves, Kitty had told him. That was a simple way of putting it. A torrent of bees zipping this way and that in her stomach and chest was a more accurate description, but nerves would suffice. Her stomach was a very small boat on a very tumultuous sea, but nerves was a decent enough summary. The skin of her face and hands alternated between hot and cold at rapid intervals, but nerves was the easiest definition.

If she swooned from all of this going to her head, she would claim nerves there, too.

It would not help matters, but it would explain them.

Why could she not move forward with confidence and calmness as so many others appeared to? Even if they were as terrified, they did not show it, nor behave in any way that might bring comment. Surely no one felt as ill as Kitty did by the prospect of dancing with strangers. How would the Season and its festivities continue if they did?

What Kitty would not give to have Prudence Vale in London at the moment. Prue had been as skittish as Kitty in her time, though now she was quite happily married and content with her station. But she had entered her confinement, and their child was to be born at their country seat rather than in London, so Kitty would have to make do on her own powers.

However weak and fleeting those powers might be.

"Remind me," Kitty managed to begin without congesting her words with the waves of nerves controlling her. "Who is Lord Eden?"

"Cousin of Lady Sterling," Izzy reminded her. "Tony's cousin's wife."

Kitty nodded, recalling the dark-haired beauty who was so fond of the Spinsters. Lord Sterling was a kind man, and Kitty had danced with him before, though she had not managed to speak much. Still, he was a man with whom a shy girl could feel safe and comfortable, which was worth remembering.

Lord Eden, however, was a mystery. A married man, so no fear for Miranda's deeds there, but married men had influence, and if Kitty did not make a favorable impression on their host…

Well, she would need to be perfection tonight, and that was that. Nothing to worry about.

At least Henshaw had promised to attend.

Her panicking heart settled a little at the recollection, and she could breathe without as much trouble as before. She might not be able to predict much else about her evening, but at least Henshaw would be there.

They had met once since his offer to attend events alongside her in order to ensure her comfort, and he had been better than his word. Not that there was much to be uncomfortable about when examining art, but his presence had gone a long way to ease her anxieties. Miranda had paraded her along the gallery at the Royal Academy, insisting that it would do a world of good for Kitty to be seen, even if she did not engage in conversation.

Kitty would walk anywhere if she did not have to talk. Henshaw knew that, and with every turn she had to make about the gallery, he offered her an encouraging smile or said something that only she could hear that was destined to make her laugh.

She had felt less on display with his smile and humor, as though he saw the true Kitty rather than whomever the others thought they were seeing. If there was nothing else promised her in Miranda's machinations, at least she'd know that Henshaw knew her.

He was her brother's closest friend, and he had become a fixture in her life in London as well. Family dinners, casual afternoons, walks or rides in Hyde Park, good company during musical evenings, or a partner in a dance in which she longed to dance. He was always there, it seemed, and without intending to, she found herself relying on him for this thing or that. Now he was officially giving her permission to rely on him, offering himself for that express purpose, and, heaven help her, she was going to do it.

She did not have to pretend anything with him, had never had cause to feel uneasy in his presence, and knew he would do everything he could to live up to all he had offered.

But what was he getting out of the venture? Surely he could not find looking after Kitty to be rewarding in his own interests. No one could possibly be that selfless. She had never heard a single instance of his being selfish or, indeed, acting in his own self-interest. Why, he had exerted himself for over a year to see to the needs and cares of Lady Edith Leveson, now Lady Edith Radcliffe, who was the sister of one of his former fellow soldiers, for no other reason than because he had been asked. Many had wondered if the pair of them would make a match after all of that, but Lady Edith had found love with Lord Radcliffe instead.

If one were to ask Henshaw, which many had done, how he felt about it, he would say that it was just as it should be, and he had never intended his interest in Lady Edith to have been taken as a courtship. But, he always added, he would only have been so fortunate as to have such a woman as his wife.

Henshaw was a remarkable man, there was no question, but how long could one who continually gave of himself and received little in return continue to be so giving?

She would make it a point to need him as little as possible, though she could not promise to never do so, in the hopes that he might take some pleasure for himself in their mutual events rather than always looking out for her. She was not a child, though she occasionally felt as uneasy as she had when she was one, and it was certainly time for her to overcome her more paralyzing shyness when in Society. That was not something anyone else could truly help her with, though many tried, as Henshaw was now.

Kitty would have to do better, and she might as well begin now. Tonight.

She was wearing a new gown for the occasion, a cream muslin sprigged with green and blue flowers in the overlay. It was hardly as fine as what others might wear to the evening, but Kitty had never been at the forefront of finery and fashion. She was pleased with it, and Izzy assured her that it was flattering and perfectly suited her.

Of course, Izzy was always saying kind things like that, so it was difficult to use her opinions as a judge.

The carriage pulled to a stop a few moments later, the light of the house filling nearly every window and welcoming every guest currently arriving for the evening. The appearance of the other ladies was not entirely clear due to the cloaks and coats covering the gowns, but Kitty's nerves began to flare anyway. Knowing that Miranda would be trying to find subtle ways for Kitty to stand out from the rest, that she would be comparing her to them, even if no one else would, that someone would have to choose to dance with her over the other young ladies present…

Oh heavens, how would she even begin to measure up to any other person in the room?

Why would anyone wish to dance with her when there were so many other fairer, more accomplished, more interesting young ladies? Who would converse with her when others would be so much more up to the task? What did she possess in nature or in looks that would draw anyone to her when the other young ladies were just as elegantly arrayed, more beautiful in appearance, and more fascinating in every respect?

She would have been better asking Miranda to arrange a match for her with someone not particularly concerned with the best of the best or fairest of the fair. Someone who only wished to find a quiet, comfortable life with someone perfectly content to be left alone. Someone respectable and perhaps just as reserved as Kitty was, who would find silence natural rather than awkward, and would not press her to be something she was not.

Did such a person exist? And would Kitty be content in not being particularly loved, but respected all the same?

Sebastian was right; she had never expressed any girlish sentiments over marriage, courtship, or love before. She had never thought much of the thing before, finding the idea of courtship too terrifying to truly contemplate. The very idea of trying to be interesting or appealing while being plagued by even more than her natural insecurities was too much to bear.

And yet…

Kitty would have been lying to herself and to anyone else if she did not admit that she had dreamed of children. Several of them, all showered with love and affection from her if not from whomever their father would have been. None of them would have felt as alone as she had felt in her youth at Lindley; she would have seen to that.

But she could not have those golden imaginations of her future without a husband, which made this pretense at courtship necessary for her, no matter how she hated it.

40

For the hope of that future, she would move forward into the den of discomfort.

Even if her knees shook with every step, as they did now stepping from the carriage.

Sebastian offered her his free arm, his other already occupied by Izzy, and Kitty fought a smile as she considered the picture they would make at being so arranged while entering. The fashions were still moderately slender enough to allow them entrance while three people wide, but if the skirts expanded any further, as they seemed to be doing with every passing year, a gentleman and one lady on his arm would struggle through a standard doorway, never mind adding another lady.

Kitty ought to have walked alone behind them, truthfully, but it was just like Sebastian to keep her safely tucked against his side rather than making the journey alone.

Would he affix himself to her the entire night too, just to make sure she was well? That would do nothing to encourage anyone at all.

They moved into the house, divesting themselves of cloaks and outerwear, then proceeded forward to greet the host and hostess. Lord Eden looked exactly like his younger brother, Mr. Demaris, though perhaps a little taller, and his wife was very warm in her welcome. Not quite a match for her husband in looks but radiating such comfort that one barely noticed.

Kitty rather liked these kinds of matches, as it made her wonder what had brought them together.

"You know my sister, Lady Eden?" she heard Sebastian ask and immediately forced a smile, curtseying in greeting.

Lady Eden's smile was almost matronly. "Miss Morton, thank you for coming this evening. If you'll permit me, I'll advise you to choose wisely for a partner in the supper set. The meal is destined to go on for quite some time."

Oh good, no pressure at all. Kitty swallowed with some difficulty. "And what if I do not dance the supper set, my lady?"

Lady Eden was completely undeterred. "Then you may sit wherever you please and among whomever you wish. Wise girl."

Ah, so not everyone was a matchmaker for unmarried women, then. She immediately liked Lady Eden a great deal more than she had upon entry.

"Thank you, my lady." Kitty let her smile spread, no longer forcing it at all.

Lady Eden winked warmly and nodded toward the ballroom. "The first of the dances is about to start, so you've arrived just in time. I must drag his lordship here out for the first, but I've promised he does not have to do more than that."

Lord Eden heaved a sigh and gave her an exasperated look. "I don't mind dancing with *you*, my love. I just don't enjoy dancing much at all."

"Which is why I do not insist upon it," she replied with a knowing smile. "Though I daresay you might request a dance with Miss Morton to ensure you are not so wholly averse to the idea."

Kitty jerked at the notion, looking at Lord Eden with wide eyes for his response.

He met her eyes, his smile surprisingly gentle. "I believe I can do that, if Miss Morton will not object to having a tepid dance partner who can only offer conversation for the experience."

Considering the man was happily married and she would not need to pretend at anything while she was with him, conversation would be welcome indeed.

"I would be pleased to, my lord," Kitty found herself answering without having to lie. "Whichever dance is the shortest so you might be free of the task all the sooner."

Lord Eden and his wife laughed, as did Sebastian and Izzy. Lord Eden bowed his acknowledgement. "Your consideration is much appreciated, Miss Morton, and I can see that it will be my favorite dance but one of the night."

"It seems it might be your only dance but one, my lord," Kitty replied easily. "But it is kind of you to say so."

She followed Sebastian and Izzy into the ballroom, grateful to not look the awkward set of three as they entered. The room was the very definition of elegant simplicity, which put her more at ease. She would not feel so out of place in here, no matter how fine the other guests looked.

"Ah, good, you're here," Miranda's voice sounded, and Kitty felt her stomach sink and her heart lurch all in one. Still, she had to smile.

"Good evening, Miranda."

Her patroness looked her up and down, nodding. "Good, good, excellent, you look lovely. Of course, you always look lovely, but it bears saying so this evening. I've a selection of gentlemen for you this evening, but not all at once. I'll walk you around a little later, and we'll meet them one at a time. I've not arranged any dances for you in advance, as it is best to let these things proceed naturally."

"Miranda…" Sebastian groaned in a low voice.

Her eyes flicked to him very briefly. "You cannot fully appreciate my restraint, dear Morton, in doing so. But this is about your sister, not me, so I have arranged nothing. Though I would not find my own evening well spent if you are not engaged for the waltz, my dear Kitty. If you would take my advice, do try to secure that dance, at least. Still, I cannot pretend to understand the ways of Society's bachelors. Heaven only knows what ineptitude lies in such creatures."

Kitty stared at this terrifying woman, this self-proclaimed societal godmother of hers, and wondered how she could say things suited to Kitty's tastes and nature and in the same breath, express her own wishes that were so against Kitty's.

From anyone else, it would have seemed a rather twisted manipulation. But from Miranda, it was simply a statement. In a way, the discrepancy was flattering, as it did show her complete understanding of Kitty's preferences, even if she wouldn't have chosen the same.

Still, even this slight push was overwhelming. Perhaps Miranda could pluck up the perfect man for Kitty and drop him in her sitting room with a ready proposal. That would have tidied up the situation rather well and would keep Kitty's nerves at a minimum.

But it could not possibly be so easy.

"How am I to know when the waltz is?" Kitty asked Miranda, lacing her fingers together to keep them from shaking. "I am not impulsive, so it would do well for there to be a plan if I've a hope of dancing it."

"Kitty," Sebastian scolded, "you do not have to dance any particular dance at all." He threw a quick glare at Miranda that was ignored.

"I am not promising I will," Kitty assured him, as well as herself.

"I am only saying that I know I cannot do it unless there is a plan."

Miranda's eyes lit up. "Clever girl. Yes, I see your point. I will go inquire of Lady Eden before she and her husband start the dance. Excuse me." She swept away without another word, leaving Kitty to breathe freely.

"Why are you indulging her?" Sebastian hissed beside her. "This is madness."

"Someone must push me," Kitty said without energy. "Heaven knows, you and I will not."

Her brother had no answer for that, and, blessedly, Izzy steered him away a moment later.

Again, Kitty exhaled a slow breath, the evening already drudging up more than she'd thought it would.

And she had yet to dance at all.

"Oh, thank heavens, I was so afraid I'd be the only person of sense in the room."

Her lungs relaxed completely, almost leaving her woozy with the sensation, and she turned with a relieved smile to face Lieutenant Henshaw, who was just coming up to her. "I am quite delighted to see you as well."

He seemed surprised, grinning at her in a way that had her stomach tightening rather strangely. "Are you?" The question was almost one of disbelief—so soft, it was sweet—but then he laughed and added to it. "What could possibly be so bad as to bring you to such depths?"

Kitty gestured faintly to their surroundings. "This, of course. Miranda has plans, and my brother is possibly as afraid for me as I am. He turned the carriage around to take us home."

Henshaw cocked his head, his brow creasing slightly. "And yet here you are."

"I made him turn back," she admitted, ducking her chin a little, her cheeks beginning to warm. "I will gain nothing by hiding at home."

"Knowing how uncomfortable you could be, you made him turn around?"

She lifted her eyes to his, his smile prompting one of her own. "I did."

He shook his head. "You see? You're braver and bolder than you think you are."

"With my brother," Kitty reminded him, laughing once. "Undoubtedly the easiest target of all."

"Well, we must all start somewhere." He chuckled and looked around the room a moment. "Miranda has plans, you say, and yet I don't see her."

Kitty rolled her eyes and gestured toward the door. "She's gone to find Lady Eden to ask when the waltz is. She plans on introducing me, or reintroducing, I'd imagine, to a few bachelors tonight, one at a time, and hoping they will ask me to dance. I suppose I should be grateful she did not fill a dance card for me, but she seems to be keeping to my preferences, for the most part. She would particularly like me to dance the waltz if I manage to be asked." She shuddered at the idea, feeling suddenly cold, and looked away.

Henshaw made a soft hum of sympathy. "You don't like the waltz?"

"I don't mind the waltz," she corrected, hedging away from the implication a little. "But this is different."

"How so?"

"I do not think I can waltz with any of the men she wants me to," Kitty confessed in a half-whisper, shaking her head. "The waltz is so close a dance, and they would be almost strangers. But if I do not dance the waltz, I'll never hear the end of it."

"Waltz with me."

Kitty jerked back to look at him, eyes wide. "What? She'd never consent."

"She is not your keeper," Henshaw reminded her, his tone soft but firm. "And you said she did not plan out dances for you, which means she is leaving you the power of your choice on the matter."

That was true, but would dancing with Henshaw defeat the purpose of the thing? She would be infinitely more comfortable, but could she really keep her own comfort at the forefront of her mind and achieve results?

Henshaw could clearly see her indecision and he smiled, raising his brows. "If you want to dance the waltz, dance it with me, Kitty. She cannot say it is a waste when I am an eligible bachelor, right?"

Kitty giggled, then covered her mouth. "That is true, isn't it? I've never thought…" She bit down on her lip and focused her eyes on Henshaw's buttons rather than his face.

"You haven't thought of me as an eligible bachelor?" he finished, his tone just as carefree and warm as ever. "That's all right, no one really does. Leaves me quite at my leisure, actually."

She looked up at him with a quick smile. "So you can save a shy girl from a waltz with a stranger by waltzing with her yourself?"

Henshaw shrugged his broad shoulders. "It is a sacrifice I am well able to endure, as the cause is true."

"How noble a knight you are!" Kitty sighed in relief and nodded. "Yes, I would much rather dance the waltz with you, thank you. Now, if only I could come up with a plan for the supper set. Lady Eden told me to choose well, and it seemed to amuse her when I suggested I would not dance it at all, but then, what if I become trapped between horrid guests for supper?"

"Again, a rather simple fix," Henshaw told her. "Don't dance it if you can avoid the thing, and I'll do the same. I can arrange to enter the dining room with you, and it will be very natural to sit beside each other. Nothing suspicious at all."

Kitty gave him a look. "Are you going to be the answer for everything all night?"

"If the answer fits," he shot back. "I told you what I'd be here for, and I intend to match my words."

She searched his eyes for a moment, a deep, rich blue she hadn't ever explored before, so full of light and laughter and, currently, sincerity. He was a handsome man, there was no question there, but somehow, in the time she had known him, that had gotten lost among everything else. It was an easy sort of handsomeness, something that grew on a person with every passing encounter, though there was certainly enough for the first look to make it worth the while. But his appearance could not match his smile, and his smile was eclipsed by his laughter. And his laughter…

Well, his laughter was music enough, but it did not hold a candle to his quiet conversation. He had a way of making a person feel as though there were no other demands on his time, no other preference in his nature, no other individual more important. And when one considered that he was handsome while doing all of that, there was no more attractive man anywhere to be found.

The thought slapped itself along every wall of her mind and her cheeks turned to flame, her eyes unable to move away from his.

Cool, blue fire in those eyes, and she was slowly burning from it. What was this madness?

"All right," she said, sounding as though from a very great distance. "I'll meet you at the dining room."

Henshaw nodded, apparently unaffected by whatever was taking her over. "Now, we must hope the waltz is not one of the first three dances, as I promised Lord Eden I would dance those to show his wife that dancing will indeed take place. If I come running for you in a frenzy in the next hour, know that I am in desperate need for a partner to fulfill my duty and kindly consent."

Kitty barked a laugh that was not quite hollow. "There are other ladies, Hensh. Charlotte Wright is just over there."

"Have you ever danced with Charlotte before?" Henshaw snorted softly. "I adore her, but it's like dancing with my most critical sister."

"Who is... ?" Kitty asked, unable to help herself.

"Billie," came the dry response. "I cannot even sneeze correctly, in her mind." He shook his head, heaving a sigh. "I'll fetch you for the waltz, unless supper comes first. Don't give my dance away."

Now Kitty laughed. "I won't."

Henshaw nodded with a smile before turning to find his partner for the first dance, leaving Kitty wondering if a waltz with him would satisfy Miranda's plans and possibly her own.

Chapter Five

The arrangement of dinner placements is critical to the success of one's evening. Imagine being placed next to a boor or a simpleton! Or, worse yet, a chatterbox who does not eat so much as inhale, somehow managing syllables around the obstacles of sustenance. The greatest dinner party this author has ever attended involved sitting beside a reticent gentleman who said little, ate steadily, and made no attempts to be charming. In doing so, he has been raised to a far superior level, and his company dearly missed. Choose wisely, dear ladies, and save yourselves.

-The Spinster Chronicles, 23 April 1816

Edward wouldn't have thought it possible, but dancing three dances in a row among the first of the evening was not enough to tire him out.

On a normal evening, he could have said they would, but tonight, they had not. Because he had a waltz with Kitty later on, and for that, he would have danced every dance leading up to it, as well as every dance after, and done all of them with a smile on his face.

Michael Sandford, Tyrone Demaris, and Edward had been recruited to dance the first three dances at Lord Eden's ball, more to assuage Lady Eden's worries about a lack of dancing than for any personal interests. Michael had agreed to the thing with the same reservation as Edward, but Tyrone had been rather irritable about the whole thing. It was not so surprising, he supposed, as it had been his brother who had asked it of him, and Tyrone did not like being told to do anything by anyone. Still, they had all done it and now were free of the duty.

Edward had made a beeline for Kitty when he had seen her come in, wanting to make certain she knew that he was dancing the first three dances out of responsibility and not out of neglect for her. He usually danced with her at every event, and he had no idea what she expected of him as far as the priority of the thing, now it was a habit. He certainly had not expected to be given the chance to offer for her in the waltz. He'd never waltzed with her before, though he'd certainly wanted to a number of times.

Tonight, he would do so.

Would wonders never cease?

His first three dances of the night had been pleasant and uneventful, which was all he could hope for from them. His partners had been excellent dancers, passable conversationalists, and sensible young ladies who would not take his request as a preface to anything more. He had chosen well, given the options at the time, and had danced perhaps twice more since then, all with known friends. He had been free of anything that would keep him from spending the rest of the evening with Kitty, and he had certainly been doing so.

He made it appear as though he was simply in the company of their mutual friends, but his heart was entirely attuned to Kitty. Every motion of her eyes, every hint of a smile, every sign of amusement brought on by the conversations around them and, in particular, anything he said or did that might make her happy.

He was utterly pathetic, and he did not even mind.

The waltz was everything, in his mind, and he would yearn for it the entire night, wondering when the time would come.

It had not come yet.

Kitty was presently on her third walk about the ballroom with Miranda, which meant she was meeting her third potential suitor. The first one had given Kitty decent conversation, according to her report, and the second, a dance, which had been fair, though watching it had been horrendous for Edward. The dancing itself had been fine enough, but Kitty had smiled and seemed at ease with her partner, much to Edward's dismay.

She had given nothing away on that one when she'd returned, which had done nothing for Edward's envy or anxiety. He could only hope this third would be an unmitigated disaster of a relatively mild status so Kitty would not be embarrassed by it.

The supper set was about to start, and she had no plans to dance it. If this interlude with whomever Miranda had selected went well, that plan could change in an instant, and Edward could have a competitor. Not that one dance was enough to dictate the entire future, but one dance and then extended conversation during a meal could give a new young man an advantage that Edward might not have.

He was fighting a completely different battle from any young buck first glimpsing Kitty's loveliness. He already knew her perfection and reveled in it, but he had to claw his way back from the pasture of friendship he had put himself into if he had any hope at all of becoming someone more than that in her eyes.

Someone she could potentially love.

Even if she could see him in that different light, there was no certainty that she would come to love him the way he wished. There were so many unknowns in this that it seemed ridiculous to even try.

But so desperately did he want a future with Kitty, and so eternal was the flame of hope within him, that he would try every day until options were exhausted and continue to hope beyond that still.

"You're staring."

Edward turned quickly, alarmed at having been caught, but was relieved to see Izzy Morton, Kitty's sister-in-law, standing there, a quiet smile on her face.

"Am I?" he murmured, relaxing slightly as he turned back to pretend he was surveying the ballroom as a whole.

"She's pleased to have you around, you know," Izzy told him, lowering her voice. "She's told me a little, mostly about how you offered to keep her company."

"That's good," he replied, something warm tingling the center of his chest. "But in what capacity, I wonder?"

Izzy sighed in sympathy. "I wish I could tell you that, Hensh. I really do. But that does not mean she will not see you as you wish. And once she does, she will see every moment she missed where your feelings were clear. Why, I've suspected for quite a long time that you felt something for her."

"And I believe you are the only one who did," Edward said, giving her a knowing look. "I credit your observation skills, Izzy, but I don't think everyone can consider my feelings as being clear."

"Whyever not?"

He snorted very softly. "I have been tied to almost every one of the Spinsters as a candidate for marriage from the moment I aligned myself with the group. Yet no one suggested the one woman I have wanted to be my wife from the moment I set eyes on her. No one else saw it, and if that does not tell you something…"

Izzy chewed her lip for a moment, her brow furrowing. "I hardly think one's potential spouse must be an obvious choice. Look at Cam and Prue."

Edward blinked at the suggestion, then laughed to himself as he considered the match of Mr. and Mrs. Vale, and the oddity it appeared from the start. "That's true. No one saw that coming."

"And why would we have?" Izzy smiled at him, now perfectly at ease. "It does not matter what anyone else sees, Hensh. Only you, and only her. And I think, if I know Kitty at all, she will see."

"And will I like what she sees?" he asked aloud, knowing she could not answer that either.

But the question remained.

"Keep trying, Hensh," Izzy encouraged, putting a hand on his arm.

He managed a rather humorless laugh. "I'm not likely to stop trying. I can't."

That, it seemed, was exactly what she wanted to hear, for her smile spread into a thing of brilliance. "I did not realize you loved her so very much. I'm delighted to know it now." She squeezed his arm and left him, moving toward her husband as the supper set began.

"If only *she* knew it," Edward mumbled to no one in particular. He looked back toward Kitty's conversation with the third bachelor, praying it had not led to a dance.

Sure enough, Kitty stood there alone, her bachelor now on the dance floor with someone else. He'd never been so delighted to see her alone in his entire life.

Her eyes met his, and their blue depths widened meaningfully while her mouth quirked with some twitch of amusement or humor.

He grinned back unabashedly, delight and relief mingling with complete adoration. Clearly, she had something to share about her most recent attempt at fulfilling Miranda's plans for her, and he could not wait to hear all about it. If it did not lead to her having a dance with the gentleman, there was no hope of it going anywhere beneficial for anyone. What sort of an idiot was a man who could spend five minutes in Kitty's company and not wish for decades more with her?

Edward's legs suddenly itched to go to her, to cross the ballroom or circumnavigate it to avoid comment and spend the length of the supper set with her so they could proceed into the dining room naturally together. But crossing to her with that kind of determination at the beginning of the set would bring with it the expectation to then join in the dance with her, which would defeat the purpose of their arrangement. So he would stand here, blatantly staring, embracing the fact that he could do so without her thinking anything peculiar about it.

And he could revel in the experience of her staring back.

It was not as though she was feeling the same things as he was in the experience, but at least he was not alone in it for once.

Something Kitty saw in his expression made her laugh, and he wondered if it was possible for a grin to actually crack his face into a million pieces. All he wanted was to make her smile and laugh, and here he had done it, just by existing. Or staring. Or whatever it was she saw.

How could he repeat something he didn't know he was doing?

Kitty flicked her eyes toward the dancing, then back at him, pointedly. Edward followed the gesture, witnessing some truly appalling attempts at dancing by the gentleman with whom Kitty had been speaking only scant minutes prior. It would not have been out of place at a pantomime of English Society on a stage or street corner, and the poor miss forced to dance with him grew more and more exasperated as the dance went on.

Edward clamped down on his lips hard, returning his attention to Kitty, whose rampant amusement might have been the most beautiful thing he had ever seen. He shook his head very slightly, then made a show of exhaling in relief for her to see.

Her chin dipped in a nod twice, her eyes widening for a moment in agreement.

Conversing across a room without words… Surely that was something reserved for people with a deep connection and history, yet he and Kitty were managing it with ease.

Could that be a sign of something? Was he desperate for hoping it was?

They continued to communicate in that manner about this thing or that throughout the supper set, and only when it ended and Lord Eden announced his request for them all to proceed into the dining room could Edward draw a full breath. He walked as casually as he could manage with the energy thrumming through his limbs, pointedly not looking for or at Kitty as he did so. Now that the attention was not on the dance, any hint of prior arrangement was far more easily sniffed out.

That was the last thing they needed.

He smiled at those around him who met his eyes, making brief but polite conversation with those he knew well enough, while moving in their same direction for the dining room. Every now and again, he would try to find Kitty to mark her progress, and she seemed to be doing just as he was, making no haste and appearing entirely at ease. Her eyes met his once, sending a jolt of pleasure into his right arm, and the slight curve of her mouth made his fingers clench ever so slightly.

And he was supposed to make it through a supper sitting beside her?

The dining room was spacious enough for a much larger party than the Edens presently had, which made for comfortable seating arrangements, and it was easy enough for Edward to make his way over to the side of the table where Kitty was heading without looking intentional.

He walked past her, stopped, pretended to look thoughtful, then turned as though he could not decide where he ought to sit for the meal.

Kitty watched him, brightening with perfect timing as he reached her. "Lieutenant Henshaw! Have you been enjoying yourself this evening?"

Edward could have burst out laughing at her cheery tone, so

unlike the shy creature he had first known her as. "I have indeed, Miss Morton. And you?"

"Oh, very much so, sir." She gestured to the table. "Will you take the seat beside me for supper?"

"Thank you." He pulled the chair out for her, then sat beside her once she was situated. "Well done," he murmured as he pulled the napkin from the table and set it in his lap. "Such a natural actress."

Kitty scoffed in surprise, her lips tightening as she fought laughter. "And I very much enjoyed your brief hesitation as to where you ought to sit for the meal. Quite believable, if I may say so."

"You may," he assured her with an incline of his head. "I have much practice with confusion over such things, so I was able to call upon my previous experiences."

"Ah, that explains the skill, then." She smiled at him, the color in her cheeks so becoming a shade, it was a wonder some artist did not immediately appear to capture it. "Thank you for doing this for me. I adore Miranda, but I think I would have died a little, had I been forced to sit beside her. She would have made me talk, and I am so tired of talking."

Edward returned her smile with as much sympathy as he could. "Her enthusiasm does her credit, but where in the world are the rest of us supposed to find such energy?"

"Exactly!" Kitty sighed noisily, shaking her head a little. "I will not pretend she is not considerate of my tastes and nature, but she does tend to push on so. It is not as though there is a need for haste in this. I am not aging before our very eyes, am I?"

"No, not at all," Edward said quickly. "You're as lovely as I have ever seen you, and no one could think anything wanting."

Kitty gave him a surprised look, her smile small. "Really? That is very kind of you to say, particularly when I feel strained."

He swallowed against being so caught in his own words, instinct telling him to recover something. But this time, he would ignore the instincts. "It is not kindness," he told her, lowering his voice. "Simply truth. And if this is you appearing strained, then the rest of us will need to find a new description for the thing. I think you're matchless, Kitty, and I don't mind saying so."

His heart stopped in his chest as the last of the words tumbled from his mouth. It was as bold as he'd ever dared to be with her, and the greatest chance he had ever taken. How would it be received? How would the rest of the evening fare because of it?

Had he ventured too far?

Kitty stared at him a long moment, then, to his astonishment, smiled almost tenderly, her color heightening just a little. "I don't know what to say," she murmured, the light in her eyes too much to bear. "If I refute you, it will only make you insistent, and if I accept it, then I am indulgent. I know you better than for you to flatter needlessly, which means it is your truth. So, how shall I respond?"

"Take it in," he suggested, managing a smile. "Say nothing. Your smile and your acknowledgement of my sincerity is more than enough."

He watched her throat move on a smile and felt three pounding beats of his heart before she looked down at her plate. "I'm feeling rather ticklish all of a sudden," she said softly, no doubt more to herself than anyone else. "Quite a peculiar sensation. Do you know it?"

"Right between your stomach and your ribs?" he inquired, as though it were a typical topic of conversation.

Kitty nodded, still not looking at him. "Just so."

Edward exhaled very slowly, as silently as possible. "Oh, yes. I am quite familiar with it. Don't despair, it will pass."

"Despair is not an accompanying feeling," she replied as she reached for her glass of water. "Rather the reverse."

He somehow managed to choke on air at that and cleared his throat rather awkwardly, nodding at the footman who was now serving up vegetables for his supper. Death was surely imminent, but at least he would have a decent meal before he perished.

"Oh, dear."

Kitty's low words, filled with true uneasiness, brought his blissful chaos to a halt. "What?"

She indicated down the table, her expression worried, and Edward saw their friend Charlotte seated beside her new potential suitor, Mr. Riley. Across the table from them sat Michael Sandford, Charlotte's best friend, and Miss Palmer, whom he was now pointedly courting. Michael had adored Charlotte for years, and the feelings were not yet returned. Now they were both pursuing courtship, and relations between them could not have been more strained.

It was an awkward situation, and Edward had shared a few words with Sandford on the subject only that evening. "Yes, that was bound to happen eventually, wasn't it?" he told Kitty with some reluctance. "I am happy Sandford is determined to find joy for himself, but somehow, I don't believe this is it."

"No, it is not," Kitty whispered, her brow creasing as she watched them. "Do you think those four people could accept moderate happiness for themselves when there is a chance of having greater than that elsewhere?"

"I don't know," he admitted. "I know Charlotte is determined to marry soon, more to save herself from loneliness than anything else, which is probably why Sandford is doing what he's doing, but as for the other two innocent parties…" He shook his head slowly. "I would be hard-pressed not to intervene, should it get that far. We must hope that they see things more clearly before then."

"Or have Miranda force them to see it," Kitty suggested, looking at him with a slight smile. "Do you think she would?"

Edward laughed with ease. "Oh, I know she would! But would you send her their direction to get her off your course more than you would for their own good?"

Kitty shrugged a little and started on her meal. "I think it would be a fairly even motivation for one or the other, but it would certainly benefit everyone in the end."

"So, why not ask her to stop?" he asked, dabbing his mouth with his napkin. "You've given it a chance, and so far, I cannot see you finding much enjoyment in it."

"Oh, I'm not," Kitty replied with a laugh. "And if I thought for a moment that I would fare any better on my own merits, and possessed even a little ounce of bravery, perhaps I would."

Edward waited a moment for her to continue. "But?" he prodded when she did not.

She flicked her eyes to him before looking down at her plate. "I've never really thought I would marry. I wanted to, of course. Wanted a family, children, a husband who cared for me… I simply did not think I would be considered a candidate for anyone, what with my shyness. But Miranda's offer, strange as it sounded at the time, has given me a chance to consider what it is that I want and what might be possible. And now... I think it might pain me forever if I am deprived of the chance."

Had he the strength of any limb in his body, Edward might have fallen to his knees and proposed right then and there to her. She would not be deprived of the chance, he would never let her be, but it was not the time to offer himself in that way. He did not want to save her from a miserable prospect; he wanted to be the choice she made because she wished for it. Did that mean he needed to allow for other prospects so that he might be a choice and not a chance? It would be deuced uncomfortable if so, but he would bear it if he must.

"I cannot believe I am even telling you this," Kitty suddenly said, straightening in her chair and tossing her hair a little. "Dreadfully uncouth, please forget it."

He would not forget it. Not until his dying day.

"Kitty," Edward said slowly, keeping his voice low, "if you believe nothing else I ever say, believe this: you will not be deprived of what you wish. It is not possible."

Color rushed into her cheeks, rather like it had last year when he first knew her. "Hensh—"

"I know," he insisted firmly, refusing to let her push this off. "I may not know much else, but this is something I know with absolute certainty. It is only a matter of time, so please, give it time."

Her lips parted, emphasizing their fullness in a maddening way, and he would swear he could hear the air from her lungs pass over them. "Yes," they suddenly whispered, driving his sanity to its ends. "I think I will."

The pit of his stomach clenched sharply, and he struggled for a time to manage a swallow. "Good," he eventually forced out.

"Which is why I need Miranda despite the discomfort," Kitty went on, her voice clearer. "Someone must do the uncomfortable things for me. I cannot be expected to have a particularly easy time in finding the love of my life, can I?"

Couldn't she, though? If she only knew how very easy it could have been, how close the chance of it was, how earnest the heart of such a man beat for her... But that was more about his own feelings than hers, and it would mean nothing if she did not feel the same.

"Well, I suppose you did not find it in Mr. Cannot-Pace-a-Pattern, did you?" Edward said in as light a tone as he could pretend, forcing a laugh to shift the conversation to something far more comfortable for them both.

She rolled her eyes and smiled around a bite of supper, her chewing speeding up pointedly.

The remainder of the meal was spent laughing too much and conversing just enough, ranging in topics from each of her three failed bachelors to their predictions for Miranda's choices for the rest of the evening, then to the alterations they would have made to the meal if they had been hosting, and ended, rather aptly, with an animated discussion on dancing in general and what each of them disliked about the enterprise.

Then it was time to return to the ballroom, per their host's invitation, and Edward walked beside Kitty as they followed the other guests in. It had been such a pleasant meal, such an enlightening and warm exchange for an extended time, that he dreaded having to part from her even for a moment. The waltz was ahead of them, but how long would he have to wait for that? It was as though the greater the distance between supper and the waltz, the less of a chance he would have at repeating either of them.

He was gripped by a sudden, irrational fear, and he would suddenly prefer facing an entire line of enemy soldiers with loaded rifles alone than to be parted from her.

What had happened to his dignity?

"Do you have any idea when the waltz is?" he asked, unable to completely hide the note of desperation in his voice.

"No," Kitty replied, her tone unreadable. "I wish I did."

His throat tightened. "Do you?" His left hand twitched and began to stray, reaching very faintly toward her.

To his utter and paralyzing amazement, he found her fingers almost at once, the fabric of their gloves grazing in a friction that robbed him of breath. The space between them was not great, but there was no reason why so slight a gesture should have brought them into connection unless she was also reaching toward him.

Heaven help him, was it possible she had done that?

Edward brushed his fingers against hers again, curling them ever so slightly to almost hook against them. Hers did the same without hesitation, tightening something around his heart as though it sat in the palm of his hand and felt those fingers itself.

No waltz could have been more powerful than this.

And yet…

He managed to swallow as they entered the ballroom fully, and their time together had to end, unless they wished for comment. "Until the waltz, then," he murmured.

"Yes," Kitty whispered, her smallest finger suddenly curling hard into his palm.

She was gone then, striding away with quick steps, not looking back at him, nor making any indication that they had been in any kind of conversation.

Now he knew death was upon him. He only prayed it would hold off until the waltz had ended.

Just in case.

Chapter Six

What does one gain from dancing the waltz? An appreciation for one's personal space. The true sense of a gentleman's dancing abilities and sense of timing. An echo of whatever his last meal was or his preferred fragrance is. And, more often than not, an awkwardly perspiring hand within a glove that is not to be removed. Would it be too much for such a dance to go back into its scandalizing corners?

-The Spinster Chronicles, 29 May 1818

What was happening to her? Everything was too hot; the room, her face, her heart, every breath that filled her lungs… Even her fingers felt hot, though they also felt like ice somehow, and she had to keep wiggling them to make certain she still had sensation in them.

She could not believe any of this. Edward Henshaw? Her brother's best friend? Her protector, her friend, her comfort? He was the one turning her into a ticklish, overheated wreck? It was the most embarrassing thing she could think of, and she had no idea how she was going to manage to waltz with him when she was destined to be red as a strawberry.

But his fingers had touched hers, too. The bizarre impulse she had felt to reach for him, to touch him, had not been as flighty an impulse as she'd thought. He'd had it as well, and she would never have suspected… never guessed…

He had called her matchless. Such a peculiar word, and one not attributed much to young ladies, but would now become the most treasured word of them all.

Matchless.

She could have said the same about him. There was no one like Edward Henshaw in all the world. If there had been, not one of them would have been eligible for more than five seconds. Which begged the question.

Why was he?

Rumors had abounded among their friends—and no doubt some of the extended circles—about him with various members of the Spinsters at one time or another, given his closeness with them and the moments he had been of particular service. Why, even Kitty had thought that he would marry Lady Edith, given he called on her to see after her welfare. But it seemed that he truly had been more about the responsibility and friendship he had claimed and nothing more, as she was now married to Lord Radcliffe.

At this moment, she was inestimably pleased that all of that had transpired so that it could lead to… what? What was any of this leading to? Or was it leading anywhere? Was Kitty simply so desperate for the idea of marriage and family, now that Miranda had forced her to look at it, that she would cling to the most convenient choice?

It did not explain why he would reach for her, but she would certainly need to watch herself to ensure she did not overstep purely out of curiosity for the sensations she was experiencing.

Two dances had passed since they had left the dining room, and she was not any calmer in body now than she had been the moment she had left Hensh's side.

Was this going to be permanent?

"Ah, there you are! It has taken me ages to find you after supper."

Kitty exhaled shortly and turned with a half-smile to face Miranda, who would be an excellent distraction from whatever madness was crowding Kitty's sanity. "I am so sorry, Miranda. I should have come in search of you."

Miranda waved a flippant hand. "Not a bit. I am not your nanny, child. If you find something here that amuses you, something that entertains, I invite you to indulge in it. Have you danced yet?"

"Not since supper," Kitty told her, though truth be told, she had not done much dancing before supper either, as Miranda's selection of bachelors had proven weak indeed in that area. The second gentleman, Mr. Torrens, had danced with her, and he had been pleasant enough, but he had vanished the moment the dance was completed, apparently disinterested in furthering any conversation or additional dances with her.

Kitty had not necessarily been disappointed by that, but it had been slightly embarrassing. Not that anyone had seen it, apart from Hensh, who had flashed her a sympathetic smile, but as for the rest…

Miranda tsked softly in disappointment. "What am I going to do about the men in England? And what of Lord Eden? Was he not to dance with you?"

"I will not hold him to that," Kitty insisted with a smile. "He is our host, after all, and has such distaste for the thing. And we did joke about it being the shortest dance of the evening."

"Which will undoubtedly be one of the country dances," Miranda said on an exhale, somehow nodding and shaking her head at the same time. "He could do a great deal for your popularity if he would look as though he enjoyed it, whichever dance it happens to be. I can get Francis to dance with you as well, though it will do nothing for your aims with bachelors."

Her aims? Miranda was the one arranging all these things; Kitty was simply following along.

"I am promised for the waltz," Kitty heard herself say before she could stop herself.

Miranda turned to her with immediate interest. "Are you indeed? With a bachelor?"

Kitty bit the inside of her cheek. "Yes."

"Someone I know?"

"Yes."

"Brava, dear girl, I cannot wait to see who it is." Miranda patted her arm rather fondly. "If I understand Lady Eden's timeline, the waltz is next, so I will leave you alone for now. When it is done, and when whatever follows settles, we shall see if you will have interest in one or two other bachelors."

Kitty gave her a bewildered look. "What do you mean by 'whatever follows', Miranda? What should follow?"

Miranda raised a slender brow. "Have you ever waltzed with

62

someone who holds even the slightest amount of romantic interest for you?"

"No…"

The older woman hummed a rather knowing laugh that did nothing for Kitty's state. "Take all the time you need afterward. There's a lovely little terrace just there, so you may take some air if you have need."

"Are you saying I shall be overcome?" Kitty asked with some alarm.

"That depends on your stamina, darling, and your feelings. Perhaps you will be fine." Miranda shrugged a little, her earbobs nearly clapping against her neck. "Do you have any romantic interest in whoever the man is? Even a slight one?"

Kitty's mouth worked as she tried to answer, somehow to deny that she had, or to minimize what she could not explain, or to give any kind of explanation about anything related to the upcoming waltz or her feelings about it. But no words would come. Not a single syllable. No answer of any kind except an awkward, gaping silence.

Miranda smiled slightly, her eyes dancing. "I see. Rather unclear, is it? Well, perhaps the waltz will be enlightening, then." She patted Kitty's arm once more and left her, taking with her any hope of further clarity in whatever minutes remained before the waltz that could apparently be so life-altering for her.

Nothing like a touch of pressure and expectation to bring an already chaotic anticipation to the level of sheer panic. She'd have fled the ballroom had she been able to feel her feet.

She could not do this. Could not experience this. Could not risk this madness pushing a good man out of her life. Could not explore whatever feelings he was making her feel. Could not think…

Could not—

"If you are not otherwise engaged, I believe this waltz to be mine."

Oh, why hadn't she run?

Kitty tried to smile at Hensh as he held his hand out, wondering why her comfort was suddenly her torment, and how such a thing could change so very quickly.

"Indeed," she murmured, placing her hand in his.

His larger hand enclosed hers, and his smile instantly faded. "You're shaking. Kitty, we don't have to do this. Shall I take you outside? Would you like a drink? I'll take you to the cardroom, if you'd rather do that, there is nothing set in stone here."

His almost urgent shift to concern for her and offering up of alternatives to their waltz did more to settle her nerves than fleeing could have done, and her smile became easier somehow. Her fluttering had not calmed, but the panic associated with it had.

"I would like to waltz," Kitty told him in a small voice, knowing he would not judge her for the volume nor the tremulousness of it. "Though I fear I may not be very good at it."

Hensh grinned, his pressure on her hand increasing gently. "Of anyone in this room, I think I may safely say that it will not matter a jot if you are, though I highly suspect you are better than you think."

"You will not be saying such nice things if I crush your toes," Kitty said as he led her toward the other dancers.

"It would take a weight far greater than yourself to cause my toes any harm," Hensh assured her without concern. "Tread on them all you like."

She laughed, more startled than anything else, so the sound was a trifle nervous, but the amusement was genuine, and she felt lighter for it. How could she feel this strange buzzing throughout her chest and somehow still laugh with him? The comfort found in him was not gone, though he was causing her torment as well. It was still there, beneath the nerves and the buzzing and the uncertainty. The comfort she had always known in him was there.

She could cling to that as she waltzed, even with all the rest. Perhaps despite all the rest.

"Don't think about anything else, Kitty," Hensh murmured as he turned to face her, his smile gentle and warm, igniting the same ticklish fire she'd felt at dinner, though now it encompassed her entire chest and began to spread down her arms. "It's only me."

Yes, it was. And tonight, for some reason, that was the best and the worst possible thing.

His hand found her waist, and she caught her breath as she reached for his shoulder, their free arms stretching overhead to grasp hands. She might have imagined it, but she thought, for a moment, that Hensh's breath faltered, too.

Was it possible that, just as before, she was not alone in this?

Her heart pounded twice, making the effort to swallow almost impossible against her parched throat.

"And it's only me," Kitty whispered, now closer to Hensh than she had ever been in her entire life, his stature somehow more impressive and imposing for her proximity, the heat of him radiating into her own body with every passing breath.

His smile grew in a manner that curled her toes in her beaded slippers. "Exactly. What could be better?"

What indeed.

Matchless, he had said before. There was no question now that this waltz would be matchless, if not breathless, senseless, reckless, and madness as well.

All of them at once and more.

They began to move, their legs brushing with the initial motions as they tried to find their way, and Kitty, for one, gasped a hitched breath at the unexpected contact. Hensh only stared at her, his blue eyes now a dark shade rather like that of the lake at Linley and twice as tempting. She could not have looked away if she had wished to.

And she very much did not wish to.

The music seemed to swell at that moment, which Hensh paired perfectly with a turn, and Kitty felt herself swept away with the combination. She was no longer in control of her body, its motions, or her own breath. There was only the pressure of his hand at her waist, the feeling of his hand grasping hers, the slight guidance that steered her as expertly as though he captained the ship that she had become. She was completely unaware of the ground beneath her feet, the air that she breathed, how her heart was pounding, or if she was, in fact, stepping on his toes.

None of that mattered. Not a single ounce of it.

There was something magical about this experience. Of being so wholly caught up in this moment, in this person, in this dance, that she ceased to exist. And yet she was here. She did breathe, her heart did beat, and her head, though it swam wildly, sat upon her shoulders just as it had before they had started.

The dark blue depths of his eyes holding her steady on him

seemed to be the actual breath of life, what kept the blood flowing through her veins, allowed her feet to move in any motion at all. How she blinked, how she followed, how she even stood upright was a complete mystery to her now.

There was only Hensh, and she was only this creature of light and nothingness in his arms.

In his arms. Had any phrase ever sounded so delicious?

The music moved again, and again they turned as though he controlled the music as well, the emotions rising within her matching everything to such perfection, it might have been a performance on the stage. Yet she had never been here before, never done this, never felt…

Hensh's chest moved on an exhale that she could feel beneath her hand, could feel racing up her arm and reverberating along every fiber of her being. His breath became her breath, the exhilaration and confusion and bewildering bliss of it all shared in the small space between them, in their connection to each other, in some unspoken bond that had nothing to do with hands or dance or movement.

It was deeper than that. Deeper than any existence Kitty could have fathomed. How did anyone manage to exist independently after something like this? Whatever it was, could it be repeated and recaptured? Could it be felt in other ways and under different circumstances? Was this one glimpse of heaven that she would never again know?

Her heart seemed to move in time with her body, though the motions were just as inexplicable there as anywhere else. Heat began to rise within her chest, lighting one rib at a time in exquisite torment, a fire that did not have ignition or fuel; it only burned.

And oh, how it burned!

She felt herself drawn closer, could feel Hensh's fingers inching along her waist the closer she came, felt her own fingers on him do the same. The tips of those fingers dug into the fabric of his jacket, grasping at him helplessly, gripping for dear life and with an abandonment that seemed shrouded in exhilaration.

His eyes widened, the color in them swirling with a beautiful ominousness she dearly wanted to explore. She felt the breath pass her lips, saw those eyes dip ever so slightly to them, and the moment they did, the fire in her ribs exploded in her stomach, somehow reaching to the soles of her feet and arching her closer.

They turned again, somehow without either of them guiding, the music lost to the fog in Kitty's ears, and yet conducting the very patterns in which they moved. She felt boneless and anchorless by now, a quivering bundle of stars glinting sporadically in curious time with the beat of her thundering heart. But no place shimmered so brilliantly as the place beneath his palm at her back and the hand which he held.

Surely he would feel every sensation that she was through those points, would grasp the madness she was so enveloped in, might see…

Might understand…

A new sound broke through the haze, tickling something in her ears. The sound of applause, which seemed apt for what had just happened, but it was also a harsh sound, something unwelcome and intruding upon such beauty.

There was no music now, and the moment she noticed that, the entire world came sharply back into focus. And with it, the ability to think and to recollect.

The ball. The waltz. The madness.

Now she blinked and felt herself do so, staring at Hensh in confusion that soon became some embarrassment that clawed at her stomach but did not reach her usually flushing cheeks for once in her life. No, her cheeks felt cold, and even as her arm lowered from above her head, still clasping Hensh's hand, she felt a wash of echoing cold that did nothing to extinguish the heat inside of her.

He stared at her in silence, expression entirely masked to the deeper feelings. His thumb began to move over her hand, as though seeking to wear down the fabric and reach the skin beneath.

Her skin tingled in anticipation.

Kitty tried for a swallow and failed twice.

Hensh swallowed and managed, his cravat bobbing with the motion. "Only us, did I say?" he whispered, only half of the words audible.

Kitty nodded, words beyond her.

His thumb rubbed her hand particularly hard just once. "Well.

Imagine that."

She'd have thought the statement almost mocking had he not followed it by bringing her hand to his lips and lingering long enough for her heart to roll over like the wheel of a carriage exactly twice.

Imagine that indeed.

Hensh exhaled as he lifted his mouth from her hand, and she could hear the stuttering nature of the sound. "Are you promised for the next dance?"

"No," Kitty breathed, wondering if he would ask her to dance again.

Did she want to die gloriously again so soon?

"M-Miranda told me to take time to recover myself," she rambled, her words still without volume. "I didn't know what she meant."

Hensh brought his eyes to hers, tilting his head ever so slightly. "And you do now?"

"Oh, yes," she exhaled in a rush. Her cheeks slowly began to heat now, reminding her that saying what she thought was mortifying, and even such a good friend as Hensh might think it amiss.

A good friend... was that what he was? Was that what she wanted him to be?

His mouth curved in the slightest smile. "You'd best recover yourself, then. Thank you, Kitty, for the most extraordinary waltz of my life."

He was *thanking* her? And was extraordinary a good or bad thing in this case?

He had kissed her hand, but was that consideration, not affection?

"Matchless?" Kitty heard herself ask, wondering what had happened to her reserve.

Hensh nodded, his smile remaining. "Quite the word. I had expected as much, but not, I think, to such heights."

Heavenly days, and she'd thought the waltz incendiary? Even conversation with him set her toes on fire, and *that* was a change. Everything this evening was a change.

But was it forever?

It took her a moment to realize they were walking now, that

Hensh was leading her from the dance floor, and it occurred to Kitty that she had no idea where she was going to go next or what she was going to do. Was that a natural result of the waltz, or simply one of being lit aflame and now reduced to embers in beaded slippers?

"Here, I believe, is where I found you," Hensh murmured, turning to face her, still holding her hand. "I trust Miranda will be here sooner than she promised, so if you wish to make a run for it, now is your chance."

Kitty giggled softly, biting down on her lip, belatedly remembering how it had felt for him to take particular attention of them, and quickly released it as her cheeks warmed.

Hensh cleared his throat, which suddenly made her wish to as well. "I'll be in the cardroom if you should need me."

She raised her eyes to his, wanting to ask a question but not knowing what exactly that question was.

"I don't know why you would," he admitted with a laugh, answering the question anyway. "But just in case."

That was adorable, and Kitty would not pretend otherwise. "All right," she replied, finally finding a voice worth hearing.

His thumb passed over her hand in a faint brush again, then his hand released her, setting her adrift for what felt like the first time in years.

She did not like being adrift. At all.

He gave her one last smile, a charming, crooked one that begged for a smile in return and then turned to walk away, heading for the cardroom.

Kitty watched him go, quite against her will and yet not at all against it. Had she ever noticed how broad and strong his shoulders were? What a dashing figure he cut, particularly when in motion? How perfectly like liquid gold his hair was? What grace he moved with despite his stature and his soldierlike ways?

As though he could hear her thoughts, Hensh suddenly looked over his shoulder back at her, his smile far more hesitant than anything she had ever seen from him. There was something about that hesitance that took her right back into the middle of the waltz, burning with a light he would surely see shining from her eyes.

He seemed a little surprised to see her staring as well, and his smile grew, as did hers. He nodded slightly, which made her laugh for some bewildering reason, and, of all things, she curtseyed.

Which made him laugh.

Which only intensified the heat of the embers that had once been her feet.

Oh, heavens, what was happening to her?

Then he was gone, and the heat ought to have been gone too, only, it remained.

Burning each and every toe.

"I would say that I know that look, but I have never seen you wear it," the voice of her friend Alice Sterling mused nearby. "What in the world has come over you?"

"I haven't the faintest idea," Kitty managed, finally managing to swallow, though it did not help the parched nature of her throat.

Alice hummed softly in thought. "One might think that Lieutenant Henshaw had something to do with that."

Kitty inhaled sharply and turned to her friend quickly. "Will you excuse me, Alice? I need... to get some air before my next dance." Without waiting for a response, Kitty moved past her, unsure if she would make for the terrace Miranda told her of or simply find some potted fern to hide behind.

It did not matter, she decided. So long as she could breathe.

Chapter Seven

F riends are dreadful things. Friends who sniff out our secrets even worse. But friends who will keep those secrets… Ah, they are the least dreadful of the bunch.

-The Spinster Chronicles, 18 December 1815

"Ask him again. I don't think he heard you."

"Three times? Even I have my limits when I am being ignored."

"That's just it. I don't think he *is* ignoring you. I doubt he knows he's doing it at all."

"Oh, very well. Hensh. Hensh. HENSHAW. Perhaps I should call him dunderdunce and see if he responds."

Edward was not deaf, much as his friends might think, but it was true that he was not paying attention to them, and therefore was not responding. His mind was far more agreeably engaged, and he was not about to interrupt his own pleasure to indulge them.

Still, their chirping was annoying.

"Stop talking," he suggested blandly. "I was enjoying the scenery of my thoughts before your squawking."

"Ah ha, so dunderdunce did work," Tony Sterling commented wryly, spinning his drink against the wood of their table slowly. "I shall correct the manner of my addressing missives to you. What do you think, Francis?"

Francis, Lord Sterling, nodded beside his cousin, giving Edward a bemused look. "I've never considered Henshaw to be such a thing, but if he will not respond to anything else—"

Edward sighed and shifted in his chair, meeting the look of each Sterling in turn. "What do you want?"

Tony snorted a laugh. "Is it really so inconvenient to be sitting here with us and be expected to carry on conversation with us?"

"Honestly? Yes, I find that very inconvenient." Edward gave him a dark look, though he knew that his pleasant dwelling on the shape and shade of Kitty Morton's eyes would not come back to his mind with the same fervency while he was in this company.

"Then why did you come?" Francis asked with apparent true curiosity. "You could have refused."

Edward debated sharing the truth with his friends, playing various versions of the truth in his mind to see which might fit best with acceptable repercussions. Finally, he shrugged a shoulder. "The Mortons were busy."

Both Sterlings laughed and Edward hid a smile, knowing neither of them would see the truth of the situation for what it was. Sebastian Morton had long been a friend of theirs, so it should only follow that Edward would spend time with him and his family just as much as he did with them. Of course, at the moment, there were no Sterling wives in this grouping, and at the club, no one would dream of bringing their wives along.

No, it would only be the men in this conversation, for good or for ill, and the distance from the woman of his heart was painful indeed.

It had been a week since the waltz he and Kitty had shared, and he'd been over to her residence every day but one, apart from today. Not specifically to see her, of course. He would never be so direct.

Though perhaps it would have been better if he had. He'd thought of proposing from the moment the waltz had finished, and only a hasty retreat to the cardroom had saved him from his impudence. He'd been unable to resist looking back once more, however, and to see Kitty staring after him, her face wreathed in the sort of dazed intensity he'd never thought possible...

How he had kept moving away from her was still a mystery.

Calling upon her the next morning had been pure impulse, and he had explained it away by claiming he needed to hear all the details of her Miranda-driven bachelor hunt from the night before. She had

Rebecca Connolly

indulged him with great detail, and they had both laughed rather heartily. Enough that Sebastian and Izzy had come to investigate, and the stories were not quite so amusing to them, but at least they smiled at the telling. Sebastian had given him a rather curious yet knowing look, and Edward had pointedly ignored it. He did not need to give Kitty's brother any insight into his attempts at subtly courting her just because the man knew he wanted to.

There were limits to one's communication with friends.

The next day, he had accompanied the three Mortons to Hyde Park, walking a good deal more than he usually would have to lengthen the amount of time with them. He had been invited to stay for dinner, which he had done, and it had felt as natural as it had ever done. Apart from a newfound heat that accompanied every desire to have Kitty look at him. He usually craved her attention, but it had never felt this flammable.

He wanted to see the breathless woman who had filled his arms for that waltz beneath the image of the composed goddess he'd always known. Glimpse the same eyes that had stared after him with such abandon rather than the serenity he was used to. Sense that beneath the calm exterior with blushing cheeks beat a rampant heart he could almost hear for himself.

He could not—would not—claim to believe that she loved him, that a simple dance was enough to shift her so far. But she was not unfeeling toward him in that respect, he had seen it. She was not always so comfortable with him anymore, but only in the best sense. She was seeing him now, in a way she had never seen him before, and it was letting him hope.

Hope in a way he had only ever dreamed.

The reality had the potential to be far more incandescent than his dreams, and that seemed impossible. But there was fancy and imagination in dreams, and reality…

Reality was simply there. But when Kitty was near, reality was bright, and it was lovely. And if his dreams could touch his reality, well, he would have to start attending church services with enough regularity and fervency to make people doubt his choice of occupation.

He could not recall precisely what weak excuses he had given for the other days he had gone to the Mortons', but he had gone all the same. There had not been any significant events for them to attend together, none that required his interference on her behalf, and he felt the loss as though it had been an intentional restriction against him.

He was craving something, anything, that did not require his obvious efforts. Something that might bring them together by someone else's workings and give Kitty something to compare him to. He could not claim to be anything special on his own, but he might be preferable by comparison to some.

He required the comparison in order to be worth her consideration. She would need to waltz with someone else to prove that their waltz had been ethereal. She would need to laugh with someone else to prove that he was more amusing. She would need to stare into someone else's eyes to see...

No, he could not go that far. He did not want her staring into anyone else's eyes. He would save that privilege for himself alone.

But for him to succeed in his greatest wish, Miranda's plan might be just as necessary. By seeing the other bachelors in London, Edward might appeal to her more. She would not think what she felt with him could be found with anyone else, or that she might find better.

Of course, if she looked extensively enough, she would find a great many men who would be better, but he could promise that no one would love her better than he would. Than he *did*. No one.

She could search the ends of the earth until the end of time, and still, he would be that one.

The fear of losing her was enough to keep his distance when he wanted so very much to confess all and beg for her hand. He had never felt so ill at ease in his life as he had the last year and a half, knowing almost at once that he loved her, finding that feeling only growing the closer they became, and to know that he could not say a word if he wished for a chance.

It had been agony, and to now see a light of faintest hope was the epitome of torment.

Patience was a virtue, but forced patience was a punishment. He was not a man of temper or haste, nor was he a man of particularly strong impulses, but he was stretched thin in this and feared he might soon break.

The only thing that truly kept him on this path of self-restraint was the prospect of the future being greater than his past.

Kitty was worth the sacrifice.

"Amazing, he's done it again. Something rather pressing must be on his mind."

"Tony, you're going to run out of friends if you keep harping so."

Edward grunted once. "Listen to the man. And besides, you were not saying anything of note."

Tony laughed once. "That is true. I am turning into my very own edition of *The Spinster Chronicles*, aren't I? Wondering if Charlotte really will take up with that Riley fellow, if Sandford will stick it out with Miss Palmer, who in the world we could find good enough for Kitty Morton—"

That one brought Edward's eyes round to his friend, and it was only much practice that kept him from reacting. "Kitty Morton? Are we starting on her so soon?"

Tony shrugged. "We're almost out of Spinsters. Capital S, so don't worry. I know Kitty isn't the other kind of spinster."

"She's not even one of the capital S ones, really," Francis pointed out, leaning back in his chair with an exhale. "On the outskirts of them, certainly, but not in. You'd be better off finding a match for my sister if you're feeling so inclined. She will take twenty years off my life."

"I don't envy you that," Edward remarked with a firm shake of his head. "No offense to Alice, but I have never met someone so fiery that was not related to me."

Francis gave him a wry look. "Would you like her to be related to you?"

Edward barked a laugh. "Not an offer, thank you. Excellent girl, marvelous family, but she would not enjoy marriage to me, and she would go to war with my sisters, and there are far more of them."

Tony joined in the laughter there, having met two of Edward's seven sisters, while Francis merely grinned in amusement. He had never met the Henshaw girls, nor was he likely to. But Tony had met Davina and Jo, and, when together, those two were quite enough.

Individually, they were among the best behaved of the bunch, but the pack of all seven of them were rabid in their own way. Edward adored them, but if he had not been the oldest, he would have been utterly terrified.

He was already fairly apprehensive when his sisters ganged up on him, as they loved to do.

No, the Henshaw family did not need more headstrong, opinionated women to join its ranks. It could dearly use some stability, if not a softening influence.

They would adore Kitty. All seven of them, in no uncertain terms, and in full accord. He could count on one hand the number of times that had happened in the past.

He had to marry her if for no other reason than that.

Though there were a thousand and three better reasons.

"Look, if you're just going to stare off into nothing, I'll go discuss a particular horse I'm eyeing with Gables over there," Tony said with a grunt of irritation. "At least there, someone will respond to me." He pushed up from the table and moved away, leaving Edward and Francis to themselves.

Edward flicked his eyes over to him as he walked away, smirking to himself.

"My cousin is an intelligent man, but he can be remarkably unobservant."

The low, wry comment from Francis had Edward glancing over at him. "Oh?"

Francis raised a brow. "He has no idea that you're in love with Kitty Morton, does he?"

Edward's boots skidded on the floor beneath him as he jerked in his seat. "What?"

"Oh, come now," Francis scolded half-heartedly, giving him a smile. "It's not as though it is a surprise to you, is it?"

"No," Edward said slowly, having no energy or impulse to deny the thing so simply stated. "I've known for ages, but I've just never heard anyone say it so directly."

Francis snorted once, taking a slow sip of his drink. "I cannot possibly be the only one aware of it."

An ironic smile formed on Edward's face. "You're not; you're just the only one confronting me."

"Fair enough. Who else knows for certain?"

This was a conversation Edward could not believe he was having, considering how long he had been keeping his feelings quiet. Even Izzy did not discuss the thing in much detail, and she had known the longest. Everything within him begged him to shut up and say nothing at all, all his habits and inclinations up in arms that he would dare speak.

But heaven help him, he was so tired of secrets.

"Izzy," Edward told Francis with a slight smile. "Morton."

"Really?" Francis grunted in approval. "Impressive, considering you'd need their approval and blessing."

"I went to them and asked already," Edward admitted easily. "To court her, I mean. Even though I haven't... I'm not..." He growled in irritation and shook his head. "Basically, I told them how I felt and that I wanted to try for her, and they said it was fine."

"Fine?" Francis repeated, laughing once. "You told your best friend you were in love with his sister, and he said it was 'fine', and nothing more?"

Edward gave him a dark look. "For someone who has been through the process of falling in love and winning the woman he sought, you have very little sympathy for someone else in the midst of it."

Francis held up his hands in a gesture of surrender. "You're right, apologies. So you got permission to pursue her. Are you pursuing her?"

There was no simple way to answer that question. Technically, he had been pursuing her from the start, though no one would see it that way but himself. He was more intentional about pursuing her now, what with the wager with Charlotte and all, but how could he admit that?

Perhaps Francis would understand it.

"Your hesitation speaks volumes."

Then again, perhaps not.

"I have," Edward argued stubbornly. "It's merely been... subtle."

Francis's expression turned completely incredulous. "Subtle

pursuit? That's not a thing, Hensh."

Edward glared stubbornly, a muscle ticking in his jaw even as his grip tightened on his tumbler. "Don't you remember how she was when she first came to London? No one could have pursued her outright and had a hope of success. I am not using subtlety for my own amusement. I am using it for her benefit."

His friend's eyes widened and his brow cleared. "Ah," he murmured, nodding slowly. "That. I see."

"Good for you," Edward replied with a quick flick of his hand. "First, I wanted her to be comfortable with me as a person. Someone she was not related to but would have her interests at heart. There would be no hope of courting her if she could not look me in the eye."

"Very true," Francis said softly, continuing to nod. "And you're taking care to court *her*, not arrange something with her brother. Admirable."

The praise made him uncomfortable, and he shifted in his seat with the twinge of it. "I don't know about that, but it seemed the most sincere approach. Anyway, I believe I achieved that, but I strayed too far. She is so comfortable with me that I might as well be invisible."

The hiss of sympathy Francis emitted told Edward the situation was as unfortunate as he feared, and he ignored the plummeting sensation in his stomach.

"Then Charlotte made me a wager," Edward went on without thinking, the sound of sympathy more encouraging than he thought. "Whoever gets married first—"

"Wait," Francis interrupted, leaning forward quickly and setting his elbow on the table. "You wagered? On marriage?"

The hiss that Edward now emitted had nothing to do with sympathy. "Yes…"

There was a long pause, and he could not bring himself to break it with a weak defense.

"You're an idiot."

That was milder than he had expected, but it was true all the same. "I know."

Francis nodded once. "Right, just so you know. So, you did a stupid thing, and it made you decide to be less subtle in your pursuit?"

"Something like that," Edward grumbled. "I don't know if it's working, but—"

"It's working," Francis overrode with such certainty that Edward fell silent. "No doubt about that."

Edward stared at him, blinking only when his eyes burned. "How in the world could you know that?"

Francis smiled with a maddening smugness and superiority. "I saw the waltz, Hensh. Neither you nor Kitty are skilled enough at acting to keep your feelings from your features entirely, and it was a full-on display there. You're not invisible now, I can promise you that."

Edward gaped at the man, waiting for him to begin laughing or apologize for the cruel joke he was surely making. He could not be serious, could not be showing Edward the glimmer of possibility that he had thought beyond consideration. He could not truly be giving voice to the hope that Edward had been doubting ever since that dance had ended.

But there was no laughter, no denial, no hint of dishonesty in the man across from him.

Which meant...

"Did anyone else see it?" Edward asked hoarsely, suddenly terrified that the entire world would know his secret and tell Kitty before she could come to any realization of her own.

"Oh, probably," Francis said without concern, "but there were a lot of couples in that particular waltz. I'd suspected your feelings before this, so I watched with vested interest and astute observation. It was not difficult to see."

Edward rubbed his brow hard, feeling conflicted in about seven ways. "Well, thank you for not outing any of that to Tony. He'd never let it lie."

Francis brushed a hand dismissively. "I would never do so. I only brought it up with you privately so you might take some encouragement from it. That and my own curiosity, which you so graciously indulged. I'd like to tell my wife, if I may."

"Of course, tell Janet, by all means. So long as you don't tell Alice." Edward shuddered at the idea, not entirely out of fun.

"Heaven forbid," Francis replied, echoing his thoughts perfectly. "I'm not even telling Hugh. I may not have much to claim over my siblings, but I daresay I have the most sense."

"You do," Edward assured him. "No question."

It was odd, but continuing the conversation that had felt rather revealing had actually made him more at ease by the end of it. No mockery, apart from what he deserved, no discouragement, which was surprising, and no opinions or offers of advice, which was much appreciated.

His pursuit of Kitty Morton did not seem so far-fetched after this conversation, which somehow made the entire thing seem more a reality. More than that, it seemed a rather good reality. A feasible one.

He felt rather encouraged in this task of his, which he had not expected from anyone. He could actually accomplish this, if Kitty was amenable.

If.

And, if Francis was to be believed, that might actually be possible.

"You do realize you've just given me encouragement that I've never had before, right?" Edward asked the man, giving him a sardonic look.

"I thought that might happen, yes," came the straightforward reply. Francis tossed the rest of his drink back, then set his glass back down with a sigh. "I might not know the lady as well as you do, but love is a perilous game, and the players deserve any encouragement there is. I saw encouraging signs, so I thought I'd share." He shrugged and smiled crookedly. "And now that you've mentioned it, I am squarely on your side for the wager against Charlotte. So, if you have need of a special license to beat her, consider me at your service. I will exert all of my influence to secure one for you."

Edward dropped his head back on a laugh before toasting his friend with the remnants of his own drink. "I will take you up on that, should we reach such heights."

Francis chuckled as he sat back, nodding. "Say 'when', by all means. The odds are in your favor, if you'll keep at it. And what would Miranda have to say about that, hmm?" He chuckled again, seeming particularly amused by the idea.

Edward, on the other hand, suddenly felt as though a boulder sank into his stomach. "Oh no."

"What?" Francis asked, still laughing at his own thoughts.

"Miranda," Edward said simply, meeting his eyes. "Did she see the waltz?"

Francis sobered now, his eyes widening. "I have no idea. I think it's likely, considering her interest in Kitty."

Edward swore under his breath, running a hand over his face. "Then she'll know."

"Probably. The question is, what will she think?"

The men exchanged looks, neither responding to the question, but the apprehension in their faces perfectly matched.

There was no telling what Miranda would think, and that was possibly the worst unknown of them all.

Chapter Eight

———— ❦❦❦ ————

There is nothing so unsettling as having one's intentions being revealed, particularly when one is unaware of them. If those who can reveal such things could also possess the intention or ability to instruct on pursuing such intentions, they would be far more useful. What good is knowing what one wants to do if one does not know how to do it?

-The Spinster Chronicles, 22 April 1818

"You look for him, you know. In every room you enter."

Kitty looked at Alice Sterling in shock as they entered the drawing room of Alice's brother Hugh's home for the evening's entertainment.

"I what?"

Alice gave her a sidelong look, smiling with some quiet amusement. "You look. For Henshaw. Every time you enter a room where you know he will be, you look for him almost at once."

"Do I?" Kitty whispered, her fingers going cold as they lay alongside her skirts while she walked. "I do not mean to…"

"Of course not," Alice soothed at once, smiling sympathetically. "I say it is quite unintentional if you do not even realize you do so. But you should mark it as a sign, Kitty. You look for him."

Kitty bit down on her lip even as her cheeks flushed. "Did I do so just now?"

"You did," Alice confirmed. "And you did it the other night at the Ingrams'. The moment you entered, looking like the perfect blossom from a rose, you were looking for him. And as though summoned from a spell, there he was."

Oh, it was mortifying, but she could see it now. She had been eager to see Hensh when she had arrived at the dinner party hosted by Grace and Aubrey, wanting to know which dance he would claim, trying to determine the best way to invite him to ask. Curious as to whether her heart would burst within her as it had done at the Edens' ball.

She had seen him almost every day in recent memory, and each time, she had felt something different. Tingling in random places on her body, unable to stop smiling even when her cheeks ached from it, feeling a trifle woozy in anticipation of his arrival, hardly able to eat after he had left.

Any combination of these symptoms might have given her the impression that she was ill, and yet she felt perfectly healthy. She would not claim to feeling *well*, considering the torrent of symptoms currently riddling her mind and body, but she could safely say that she was healthy.

What exactly she was, then, was far less clear.

"Which means, of course, that he was looking for you as well."

Kitty's attention snapped to her friend at once in shock. "I beg your pardon?"

Alice seemed surprised by her surprise. "He… Kitty, he could only appear so soon after your arrival if he had been waiting for you. Looking for you. Tell me, do you always see Lieutenant Henshaw so soon after arriving somewhere?"

"I…" Kitty started, her lips moving in an attempt to form more words, though she did not know which ones. There was nothing to finish the sentence with, and she looked away, racking her mind for memories to support either side of the argument.

Dinners, dances, friendly gatherings, outings of all sorts. She could not say that he had been immediately present upon her arrival, but he did seem to appear within a short amount of time, particularly of late. He did not always single her out, especially in the early days she had known him, but recently…

Her eyes widened as a new realization dawned.

"Oh, good heavens," she breathed, slowly looking back at Alice. "Do you think that he…?"

Alice took her hand at once, no doubt seeing the panic rise up that Kitty was starting to feel. "I cannot say," she told Kitty very calmly. "I don't know Hensh well enough to venture that far. But if you are looking for him, and he is looking for you, then it very well could follow that…" She smiled and squeezed her hand. "For what it is worth, I believe the pair of you would make a very fine match. If you wish it, of course."

Kitty stared at her, not quite in horror, not quite in amazement, but in some murky sense of in-between emotion that did not have a clear definition or category. Did she wish it? Did she want to pursue these confusing glimpses of exhilaration that only Hensh had ever given her? Did she want to allow herself to feel fluttery and giggly without knowing what it meant?

Did she…?

"Have you ever been in love, Alice?" Kitty whispered as her heart scampered unsteadily.

Alice sobered at once, a flash of pain crossing her features. "No, though I certainly thought what I felt was love. Don't you remember what happened last year?"

Kitty winced and hugged her friend quickly. "I am so sorry, I forgot. Please, forgive me."

"Nothing to be forgiven," Alice insisted, pulling back with a small smile. "I was naive and silly, but I thought he loved me, and I thought I loved him. I know now that was not it at all, and what I felt after I was saved was more akin to embarrassment than heartbreak. Surely if it had been love, it would have been the other way around. It would have been deeper. Not just exciting, but defining, I suppose. I don't even know if that makes any sense."

It *did* make sense, which was the most terrifying part for Kitty. It not only made sense, but it rang true.

The waltz with Hensh had been exciting. Seeing him now was exciting. Conversing with him was exciting. But all those things and more were deeper than simple entertainment. Defining… Yes, it did feel as though Kitty was defining herself with each passing flutter Hensh created in her chest. With every meeting of eyes that made her breath catch. With every dreamy thought she had no desire to cease, with every smile for no reason at all, with each and every wish she had for him to hold her hand in the same manner he had done that night at the Eden ball, she felt more perfectly Kitty Morton than she had ever been in her entire life.

Defining.

"How will I know?" Kitty murmured to herself, shaking her head, no longer aware of anything around her. "If this… if he… if I… could it be love, Alice?"

Alice patted her hand gently. "I know you, dear Kitty, and I know Hensh, too. I will not speak in absolutes, but I think you can be sure that it *could* be love. I will leave it up to the two of you to see if it *will* be love." She winked and then moved away from Kitty, releasing her hand and going to speak to Elinor, their mutual friend and Alice's sister-in-law.

Kitty stood there for a long while, staring off at nothing, not even looking at her friends, completely unsure what she ought to do next.

Her brother was in conversation with other gentlemen on one side of the room, and Izzy was at a card table with Emma Partlowe, Elinor's sister and one of Izzy's oldest friends. She could not bear to look around, for fear that she would see Hensh.

Which she dearly wanted to do.

But what would happen to her when she did see him? Would her heart soar to untold depths? Would hope choke her and steal her breath? Would her toes tingle with the maddening attraction that only grew with greater frequency of looking at him?

Would she feel anything at all, in light of the panic Alice's words had generated?

Oh, heavens, what if she felt nothing?

She could not bear it if all of this came to nothing. What use was feeling more alive if it did not last?

She did not want to go back, did not want to feel like a shadow of sorts or some witness to life but never a participant in it. She did not want to be ruled by fear anymore, she wanted to be moved by love.

Love…

She would never know if it was love if she did not see Hensh, did not talk to him, did not feel what she was afraid of feeling. Which meant she needed to intentionally look for Hensh.

If he was already here.

And wait for him if he was not.

Kitty exhaled slowly, her lungs quivering with the breath, and swallowed before turning her head and beginning to cast her eyes about the room.

Several people she recognized smiled at her and others ignored her, which was all well and good. She was not a chatterbox and did not care for polite conversation with those she barely knew. She wanted enjoyable discussions with people she liked, even if the topics were meaningless. If she were going to speak, she wanted whatever she said to mean something to someone.

If Hensh could possibly be interested in her, in any regard, he might place value on her words. If the manner in which he looked at her during their waltz meant anything, he just might.

They had danced together at the Ingrams' dinner party, but it had been different from that incomparable waltz. A quadrille, wherein he had made her giggle with his continued commentary of the other dancers, and a country dance where they had both been full of laughter and he had praised the sound of her laugh and the turn of her smile all throughout. In short, it had been enough to make her feel alight in a new and rather shimmering way.

And she wanted more of that. More of the way that Hensh made her feel. More familiarity and light. More brilliance and beauty. More breathlessness and burning.

She wanted…

She *wanted!*

She wanted to be in love, whether it was with Hensh or with someone else, though to have it be Hensh would be magical. She wanted to marry and to have children. She wanted all of that, what she had never particularly thought of before, and she wanted it with a fierceness that made her ache.

She had never known that for certain until Hensh had made her feel this way.

And she would not be truly happy without it. Could not be.

But was Hensh the answer? Could he be? Did she want him to be?

So many questions swirled about her mind, and, for now, only

Hensh would have the answers if answers were to be found.

Then, suddenly, he was there, standing along a wall nearby, and he was smiling at her.

Had he been watching her look for him? Could he know she had been looking for him?

A series of sparks began to burst in her stomach, but with them also came the familiar warmth that being with him had always provided her, even before this new madness had come about.

And that warmth made her smile, just as it always had, and the smile made her feet move toward him despite the panic living within her.

"Were you just going to let me look about the room until I found you?" Kitty asked as she reached him, pleased by the amusement that mingled with strength in her voice. "Gawking like a child lost in a fair?"

Hensh grinned at her accusation, his brows raising. "Let you?" he repeated with a light laugh. "How was I to know you were looking for me? You could have been looking for anyone, and why should I foist my company upon you if you wished for someone else?"

"As though it would ever be a trial to endure you," Kitty replied, scoffing a little and shaking her head. "Surely you know my preferences better than that."

A new light entered his eyes, something that darkened their lovely depths in a way she had seen before and was coming to like very much. "I meet your preferences? Well, that is the very highest of praise, I think. You must know… That is, surely it is clear that you meet with mine as well?"

Oh, her cheeks ought to have burst into flame at that, but instead, they only tingled with a faint heat while her heart seemed to possess the only fire within her.

Habit told her to demur and say something modest if not shy. But something new within her spine gave her a new impulse.

"You are one of the most affable, congenial men I have ever known, Hensh," Kitty told him fondly. "I have yet to know anyone who did not meet your preferences, as you are so good and find favor with so many."

"But that does not mean—" He cut himself off, looking down

at the ground and pursing his lips a little.

Kitty watched with interest as he seemed to struggle with what he wished to say, which Hensh never did. At least, not with her. He always seemed to know what to say and said it all perfectly.

What was this?

"Enduring company," he finally said, "even with a smile, is not the same as enjoying it." He raised his eyes to hers, his lips not quite forming a smile but coming close. "You are among the rarest of company for me. Company that not only meets my preferences but far exceeds them. Your company, Kitty, brings me joy, and I am not congenial enough to say that to more than one person."

Her mouth parted in surprise, her heart beating in the oddest pattern. Quick beats and then slow, soft beats and then hard. Skipping and galloping and somehow also waltzing slowly among her ribs.

No one had *ever* praised her company in any way, and he had just said… He had just…

Matchless.

The word echoed throughout her mind like a shout in marble halls, then fell like a shooting star into the pit of her stomach. That was what he was saying to her in all of this. Telling her again in the most beautiful way.

He thought she was matchless.

Hensh smiled at her fully now, her silence somehow not putting him off or creating awkwardness between them. His eyes darted down to her hands, then back up. "Something wrong with your gloves? You keep rubbing your fingers together as though they are uncomfortable."

Kitty glanced down at her fingers, unsure what he was talking about, but sure enough, they rubbed together anxiously, which she had not realized. In her haze of thoughts, her realization of what he had been saying, her tingling fingers had moved of their own accord.

And he had noticed.

Did he know why they were doing that? Was he blaming her gloves for politeness? For teasing? For…?

What did it matter what he was bringing it up for?

She raised her hand and showed it to him, the trembling noticeable. "Just the usual uncomfortable nature of them."

"My word," he said softly, his voice filled with kindness and concern. "Kitty!" He took her hand in both of his, holding tightly. "What's put you in such a state?"

Bless him, he thought she was so distressed that she trembled. Perhaps once she might have been, but this had nothing to do with distress.

Not this time.

"Oh, this and that," Kitty told him, trying to dismiss his gentle concern with as much warmth as possible. "One never knows the exact reason; I am trying to accept that reason is not always important."

He smiled then, his thumbs rubbing the back of her hand gently. "A wise notion. Will you sit with me?" He gestured toward a pair of chairs nearby. "At least until a card table opens up, should you have any ideas of playing."

Kitty nodded, her fingers flicking a little in his hold. "I have never truly enjoyed cards, actually. I came because of my friendship with Elinor, but I would not mind it if I did not play a single hand."

"Fair enough." Hensh led her over to the chairs, keeping her hand in his while she sat, then sat beside her.

Still holding her hand.

"You, however," Kitty said, turning to face him with a smile, "do enjoy cards. And Sebastian has said that you are quite good."

Hensh snorted a wry laugh, shaking his head, the thumb of the hand still holding hers brushing over the top of her glove absently. "I am a passable cardplayer. Your brother is a terrible one, which is why I appear good by comparison, but it is only by comparison, I assure you."

Kitty giggled and looked to the far side of the room where her brother was still in conversation. "Poor Sebastian. He is no cardplayer. Any victory in his hands would show itself on his face for certain."

"Whereas I am a much better liar," Hensh said with a soft laugh. "No one would suspect a thing."

"I didn't say that," Kitty retorted, giving him a scolding look.

Hensh grinned shamelessly and shrugged. "But it is the truth. I bluff better than your brother, and that's all there is to it."

Kitty shook her head, sighing playfully. "If I wanted to talk about my brother, Hensh, I could have sat with him."

"But you're seated with me," he murmured, his smile softening. "So, what should we talk about?"

What she *wanted* to talk about was how her feelings toward him were changing at a pace that she could barely keep up with. She wanted to ask him what else he saw in her that was matchless. She wanted to talk about the way his voice dipped lower and rasped when he was with her sometimes, and what it did to the back of her knees. She wanted to talk about the dreams of the future she was starting to see, and that he was starting to be in them.

But those were things she could not say. Not because of her shyness or her reserve or anything else in her nature.

It was simply not the way of things. A forward young lady was the least attractive kind, and there was nothing Kitty wanted more than to be attractive to Edward Henshaw.

Because she was growing more certain with every passing brush of his thumb over her hand that she was in love with him.

How did one say such things in a polite manner when ladies did not say it directly? Speaking her thoughts had never been particularly easy for Kitty, even when she was a child, but she could not bear to leave these thoughts, these words, these feelings unsaid.

But she could write them. Not directly, not in a letter to him or anything so bold, even in privacy. She could write something for *The Spinster Chronicles*, hidden behind anonymity and wording things in a way that would not seem a declaration. Some careful confession that would not name any particulars but would have a clear message if he was paying attention enough.

If this were what she hoped it was, and he felt as she felt.

If.

And if not, all that would be lost to her would be a column on a newssheet that might resonate with other young ladies who could not speak as freely as they wished. It would not heal a broken heart, but it would do some good.

With nothing left to her at this moment, Kitty laced her fingers between Hensh's. "I haven't the faintest idea what to talk about, actually." She smiled and shrugged lightly, managing a laugh. "Do your sisters play cards?"

His eyes widened at the change in their hands, but he held fast to her. "Most of them," he said in a slightly unsteady voice. "Franny is the best, but I am fairly certain she cheats…"

Chapter Nine

———— ⌘ ————

What is a young lady in possession of strong feelings toward an eligible man supposed to do in order to express herself clearly? Society dictates moderation, restraint, and superficial subjects alone for their misses of accomplishment and breeding, yet if one were to venture outside of the higher circles, they would find far more freedom in language for the females. Why should they be free to express the emotions of their heart and not the rest of us? What can be so indelicate about telling one's particularly treasured gentleman that he is utterly matchless? Yet any young woman in possession of such feelings must wait for the gentleman to make his feelings and intentions known before she may say anything of the sort, and even then, even after a wordless waltz that shakes her core, she must continue to guard what she says. The gentleman holds all the cards, and the young lady merely looks about the room in the hopes that she meets with his preferences enough to be approached by him. That he will say enough that she may also speak. That she could be as matchless to him as he is to her. But words are not given to young ladies in these matters. And so, they wait, poor dears, and silently yearn for the chance to receive a voice.

-The Spinster Chronicles, 17 May 1820

He had been a trifle late in reading his issue of *The Spinster Chronicles* that day, which might not have bothered Edward had the main article not been the most brilliant piece of literature he had read in his entire life.

There was no question in his mind that Kitty had written it, though there were no names attached, as usual. But he knew she had written before, and when he had read the word matchless…

That was Kitty writing, and she was writing to him. She found *him* matchless. She considered him a particularly treasured gentleman. She was waiting for him to make his feelings known to say anything, except she had written. She had told the world that she had feelings for him without naming either of them.

This was some impossible blend of heaven and hell, and he was walking on clouds while his feet were also somehow bearing twice their usual weight as he marched toward the Mortons' house.

He had left his quarters in a flurry once he had read the article, barely making it halfway through the article before he had shot to his feet. The rest of the words had somehow made their way into his mind while he'd scrambled, but the only things that seemed to linger had been the words that had called to him.

Cards. Preference. Matchless. Waltz.

She wanted to say things to him, things he had only dreamed of, and he wanted nothing more than to hear them. Now. This minute. Every minute of every hour of every single day for the rest of his life.

There would be no more waiting if this was true. If what she had written meant what he thought it did. If she had been the one to write it. Or if someone else had written it on her behalf. There were too many moments of private significance referenced in it for him to be entirely mistaken. It could not be a coincidence. Could not mean anything else.

And he could not wait.

His heart beat within him—much like thunder—with a bewildering fury he had never known before. There was no keeping pace with it, no slowing it, no hope of finding calm intentionally. He would have to let it ride out with whatever tide took him or find a way to live with the new and unsettling manner of its workings.

Until he saw Kitty, until he confirmed any of this, he had no doubt it was going to remain unsettling.

He reached the Mortons' home and was let in without any question, being such a frequent guest that he could have had a room all his own within it.

"Where is Miss Morton?" he demanded without any sort of preamble, suddenly seeming to pant with the effort of getting there in haste. "I need to speak with her."

The butler was unimpressed by either his energy or his sudden breathlessness. "Miss Morton is not at home, sir. She has gone out with Mrs. Morton to meet some of their acquaintances."

That was the worst thing he had ever heard, given his present heightened anxieties and energy, and he stared at the butler with an unexpected irritation. As though the man was intentionally keeping Kitty from him, or that he had somehow known Edward would be coming and had sent Kitty out before he had arrived. As though he could somehow make Kitty appear from thin air and was choosing not to.

How could she not be at home?

Didn't she know that he would come running the moment he read the article? Could she not understand how long he had wished for a sign such as this? What could possibly have possessed her to leave the house at any point in time? She ought to have been watching for him to come, waiting for his grand entrance to declare his undying love for her and put an end to their mutual misery.

She was *out?*

Edward finally managed to blink, and his lungs seemed to be moving in and out just as they normally did, though his feet seemed to have disappeared somehow. "Is… Mr. Morton at home?" he managed to ask, trying not to make it sound ridiculous.

The butler's expression did not change. "He is, sir. He is in his study if you wish to seek him out."

"Fine," Edward murmured, nodding absently and flicking his hand in acknowledgement. "Thank you."

He started down the corridor as the other man disappeared to other places in the house to do whatever it was butlers did when out of sight.

Talking with his friend when he wanted to propose to his sister was not a comparable alternative, and there would be no joy in it. Likely not any progress from it either, but he would do whatever he could manage to not ruin the chances he would need when he did speak with Kitty. Sebastian had already given his permission for Edward to pursue Kitty, so there should, in theory, be no issues in taking that one step further.

If all this went the way Edward wanted, the two of them would be brothers-in-law, and what man did not wish to have friends as family?

He thought back on the friends he had in his life, and he immediately shook his head. He would have taken the head off any of his friends who had tried for his sisters, and it was only luck that had kept him from dealing with such things. Keeping his friends away from Bristol, for one, and telling unflattering stories of them to his sisters for another. He would make sure to speak poorly of them the next time he went home, just to make sure.

Would Sebastian feel that way? Would he have wished that Kitty had not grown interested in Edward and tell him off in his own way? Had he hoped this interest would be fleeting and come to nothing?

He was overthinking, and he knew it. There was no help for it. He could not speak to the woman he loved about how he felt and what he wanted to offer her, and instead had to tell her brother.

That was the epitome of disappointment.

Best to approach it as he would have done, without the panic and passion.

"Morton!" he called as he neared the study, his voice echoing more than he thought it would. "Morton!"

"For pity's sake, Hensh, neither of us are deaf!" came the response from a few rooms away. "Don't come in if you're angry."

Anger was not one of his present emotions, ironically enough, and he managed to smile at the order. "I am never angry."

He rounded into the study, brow raised in a dare for his friend.

Sebastian met his eyes without emotion. "That is a lie, and we both know it." He rose from his chair and pressed his hands into the desk, his eyes falling to the paper in Edward's hand before darting back to his. "What do you have there?"

"The *Chronicles*." He cleared his throat, looking down at the pages. "I think Kitty wrote in it again."

"Probably," her brother answered calmly. "She's quite a good writer and expresses herself more truthfully that way."

More truthfully? There was even more hope than he'd thought possible in those words, and it was only through taking a slow breath he managed not to make a sound.

"Do you know if she did write in this particular issue?" Edward inquired, forcing his voice to remain steady and unaffected.

"I suspect she did, based on conversations I've overheard bits of between her and Izzy," Sebastian told him, a hint of amusement beginning to enter his tone. "Why? Something interesting in it?"

Now *that* was pushing too far for nonchalance, and Edward raised the sheet, pointing it at him. "If this means what I think it does, I'm proposing to your sister tonight."

Sebastian barely raised a brow, his mouth quirking in a hint of a smile. "Are you asking for my permission, or my blessing?"

Edward snorted once. "Honestly, neither. If she'll have me, I don't care what anyone else thinks."

The man across from him grinned, which was a rarity for him, and more encouraging than Edward could say. "Fair enough. You have both, for what it's worth."

He tried for his own version of nonchalance, nodding once. "Marvelous. Should I wait for her, or...?"

Sebastian shook his head. "She'll be a while, and then there's the Sterlings' ball this evening. Talk to her there; I am sure Francis and Janet would love that."

Edward smiled at that. "I have no doubt they will. Francis knows how I feel, which means Janet does too. If I have trouble finding a moment, I am sure they could arrange something."

"Undoubtedly," Sebastian agreed, straightening and folding his arms. "You know Charlotte isn't well, yes? Izzy thinks it has something to do with Sandford and his interest in Miss Palmer..."

"I wondered." Edward hissed, shaking his head. "Do you ever wish two people would just snap out of their idiocy and see what is right before their eyes?"

"Yes, as a matter of fact, I do."

Edward glanced at him, finding a smug, knowing look there.

That was not what he'd meant, and he was suddenly rather uncomfortable witnessing it.

"You won't object to having me as a brother-in-law?" Edward grumbled, shifting where he stood.

Sebastian shrugged. "Not particularly. I've wondered what sort of man Kitty would want for herself for years now, been terrified of the prospect and worried that she might choose someone I could not approve of, or that she would trust too easily, or…" He shook his head, exhaling roughly. "I imagined all of the worst scenarios London and Society could bring to my mind and, I am happy to say, you did not feature in any of them. From a logical standpoint, you are well-situated and financially stable. Your reputation is impeccable, and your family respectable. More than that, I know your parents, and I know they will love Kitty, which is all any older brother could wish for in these things."

All? That was all he could wish for? Wasn't he forgetting something?

"Oh, and then there is the fact that, if your intuition is serving you well, my sister will be so deliriously happy to be marrying you that she might never stop smiling for the rest of her life." Sebastian cleared his throat, grinning once more. "That helps, as well."

"Do you think she loves me?" Edward asked before he could stop himself.

Sebastian gave him a sardonic look. "I didn't exactly ask her over breakfast, but I did read the article you are clutching as though someone will take it from you. All I can say is, if you see yourself in that, I think she just might."

Edward swallowed the jolt of hope racing up and down his throat. "I love her, you know."

"I thought you might." He smiled at Edward almost wryly. "I wouldn't have let you within twenty-five feet of her in a courting sense had I thought otherwise. There was never any question that I would refuse any match for my sister that was not founded on love or friendship, and I very much hoped for both. In that sense, you might be the best I could have wished for her."

Oddly touched, Edward returned the smile. "That is, without question, the nicest thing you have ever said to or about me."

His friend scoffed a little. "Don't get used to it. I will be highly critical of anything and everything you do in regards to my sister for the rest of your life, so be prepared to answer for it. If she accepts you, of course. There is still that obstacle for you."

"I know," Edward mumbled, rubbing the back of his head anxiously. "And I grow less convinced of it by the second."

"Of asking her?"

"Of being correct. What if I'm wrong?"

"Then she'll refuse you, which she would do kindly, and we all move on. What do you have to lose?"

Only pride, hopes, and dreams, but at this point, he was willing to risk all three for the chance.

And tonight, he would do so.

Clawing the walls of his quarters had never been so appealing as it had been from the time he had left the Mortons' home until the time he had departed for the Sterlings' ball. Waiting for the chance to see Kitty, to look into her eyes and see if his feelings were returned, to find out, once and for all, if he could ask the question that he had been dying to from the moment he first saw her. If he could be part of her future, could make her happy, could fulfill her dreams, could keep her smiling for the rest of their days…

Despite all the nerves, all the anxieties, all the energy that had been trapped within him, there was also this bewildering and inexplicable joy. He did not even have her answer yet, but he was filled with this warmth that eclipsed anything he had previously known. He had never felt so exhilarated, so certain of his course, and yet so terrified of the response to that course. He could not think of what he would do if he was wrong, if she should refuse him, if he was venturing too far. He would not think of it. He had to ask her. Had to know. If she had written it, and meant him…

He suddenly felt all the frustrations she, or the writer, had expressed in the article, cursed the very same restraints that were imposed on women that kept him from being certain in this. It was bad enough for his sisters to feel muzzled, but when someone was as shy as Kitty, words were difficult enough. If she felt something strongly enough to want to express it, that was monumental. To have such a precious thing stifled because it was not done…

He'd never hated anything so quickly with such vehemence as this. But it would all be over soon, one way or the other, and his life would change regardless.

The Sterlings had outdone themselves by way of décor, but Edward couldn't be bothered to look around at it as he entered. There was only one beautiful sight he wanted to see, and he would not rest easy until he saw her.

He caught sight of Lord and Lady Radcliffe, apparently returned to London. He would have to greet and chat with them at some point, given his history with Edith prior to her marriage, but that could wait. Camden and Prudence Vale were near them, and their return was also surprising, given they had only just had a baby, but he supposed Charlotte being dramatically unwell, for whatever reason, had prompted their return. All the Spinsters reunited, then, if Charlotte could bring herself to attend.

That would make proposing to Kitty interesting. She adored each of them, and now they would all be here.

Was that better or worse?

Just as he had done weeks ago at the theater, Edward began looking for Izzy's copper hair, hoping it would lead him to Kitty. He found her in short order, in the same company as her friends, looking rather lovely in pale green. He cast his eyes over the group of Spinsters, but Kitty did not seem to be among them.

He looked around the dance floor, his heart skipping with a sharp pain. But no, she was not there either, which was a relief, though it was short-lived.

"Where are you?" he whispered to himself, now looking for Miranda instead. "Where are you?"

Miranda, as it turned out, was not difficult to find. One only had to look for a gathering of people around one particular focal point, and there she would be. The woman simply attracted attention and admiration wherever she went, and if she were not maneuvering the room for her own amusement, she would be entertaining within it.

Edward almost missed her among the cluster of people surrounding Miranda. With Kitty being her little project, it was not surprising that she would be in the same gathering, but there she was, hovering just at the fringes, though close enough to Miranda that he assumed she had been ordered to stay put. And once he caught sight of Kitty, he could not look away. She was wreathed in a silvery blue that seemed plucked from the sky on a winter's day, shimmering where she stood, her dark hair curled and coiled in the most tempting manner known to man, pearl and silver pins somehow keeping the locks from streaming down about her shoulders.

And she was looking at him. Smiling.

He moved at once, starting toward her, not caring if the entire room saw him moving in her direction. He hoped he was smiling, though he could not say if he was. At the present, he could not feel his face.

"Miss Morton," he managed to say when he reached her, his voice sounding almost strangled. "Would you dance the next with me?"

Kitty's eyes were bright, and her smile ended his life as he had known it. "Yes, of course. I would be delighted."

Oh, heavens, so would he.

"What's going on?" Miranda chirped, interrupting whatever conversation around her to look at them both.

Edward met her eyes squarely. "I'm going to dance with Miss Morton, Miranda."

One pert brow rose, and prim lips curved in a shockingly knowing smile. "I think that is a very good idea. Do enjoy yourselves."

What in the world...?

Kitty slipped her hand into his, startling him out of his surprise, and he glanced down at her, only knowing he was grinning because of the pain currently screeching into his cheekbones.

"Shall we?" Kitty murmured, tilting her head toward the floor.

He nodded, struggling for words to match his emotions, but his hand gripped hers and they started toward the dance, where couples were leaving and new couples arriving.

"Did you mean to dance a country dance with me?" Kitty asked with a small laugh.

"I'd have danced a reel if it meant a dance with you," he said without any hesitation whatsoever, giving her a direct look as they took their places.

Rosiness began to enter her cheeks then, and it bore the glory of sunrise in it. "I see," she replied very softly, and, for a moment, he thought her eyes would drop to the floor or the buttons on his jacket.

But they did not. They remained steady on his own.

Hope shot his heart to the center of his throat as the music struck up.

The ladies made the first move in this dance, and he cleared his throat as Kitty approached him. "I saw something rather interesting today," he commented as easily as he could manage.

"Did you?" she asked as she curtseyed then moved backward.

He nodded, starting forward with the other gentlemen. "In the papers, as it happens." He quirked a brow as he bowed with the rest, then started backward. "A most intriguing article offering a new perspective on the ability of ladies to speak their minds."

"Or not speak their minds," Kitty quipped, clamping down on her lips hard the moment she did so, her eyes widening.

Edward smiled rather slowly as they started toward each other, the pattern causing them to cross and circle before returning back. "Ah, so you read the *Chronicles* today. I wondered if you were aware of it. Struck a chord with me, that did."

"Really?" Her sweet voice was soft, almost childlike, yet so filled with the same hope pulsing through his veins.

He nodded, passing behind her, feeling the heat of her cross his back before they would retreat back to their places. "Yes. It sounded so familiar, so intimate and personal… Almost as though it was written for me."

Kitty's eyes were steady on him as they reached their respective lines, forced to wait for other couples to move down the line of them before they could do anything. "And if it was?"

All sensation disappeared from his right leg, and only habit kept it standing upright. "Then I would tell the writer that I adored every word, and I want to hear anything and everything she wished to say. I would tell her…" He glanced up the line, noting where the lead couples were, and how soon he could be close to Kitty.

To his relief, the lines of both men and women moved toward each other, closing the distance for each partner to take hands.

He returned his eyes to Kitty, who was utterly rapt, her lips parted, and the closer he got, the more unsteady her breaths became.

He could match her in that.

"I would tell her," he said again, dropping his voice as they took

101

hands, "that I have been in love with her for so long, I cannot remember how it felt not to."

He caught her sharp intake of breath, felt the sudden clenching on his hands as they slowly turned in pattern.

"I would then like to tell her," he went on as they stopped in place, then turned in the other direction, "that it would make me the happiest of men if she would marry me. But, I suspect, I would need to give her a chance to say something before I got that far."

Kitty's eyes were utterly luminous in the candlelight of the ballroom, carrying starlight within their lovely depths, and her perfectly full lips began to turn up just at the edges.

The dance next had the gentlemen and ladies taking hands of those beside them and turning in groups of three, so they could only gaze upon each other as they moved with the rest. It felt almost dreamlike to watch her after what he'd said, to see the beauty of her smile pointedly given in his direction, to witness the softness in her eyes, to see confidence in her being that he'd always felt was possible but was so rarely glimpsed by the public. Had his love for her done this? Had her feelings for him given that to her? Had this journey of theirs, long and complicated as it had been, given her courage to carry herself anew?

Was any woman in the world so captivating, so breathtaking, so brilliant that it was impossible to be unmoved in her presence?

Returned to their lines, couples were once again moving toward each other, one hand extended for the other.

"I don't think she would need much of a chance to respond," Kitty told him in the breath before their hands touched. "She'd only tell you that she adores you and only wants the future you are part of."

Edward clutched her hand as they turned, suddenly in agony that they had to part to round the people to one side of them before returning to each other. "Would she?" he whispered when they came back together, no longer in control of this conversation and offering everything it was, everything *he* was, to her alone to do with what she will.

Kitty nodded quickly, her eyes seeming to swim as she took his hand. "She would. She does. And she wants you to ask her."

He'd have taken her from the floor then if he thought he could get away with it. But they parted with the pattern, as they must, and he stared at her in wonder, certain his heart was now beating within her rather than within him.

"Will you?" he asked, knowing she would see him ask more than hear him. He could not wait until they were together again, afraid he would wake from this moment.

Kitty beamed with the glory of the dawn, stealing whatever remained of his breath. "Yes," her mouth said, the word silent, but the nod that followed echoing it.

Edward gaped at her shamelessly, certain someone was going to begin mocking him for believing any of this was true. But there was only Kitty there, and she was not laughing at him nor teasing. She was beaming at him, just as he'd always dreamed she would. Her expression was filled with the exact warmth and adoration that had so long resided in his heart. Her fingers were rubbing against one another at her sides, and this time, he did not pretend to suspect her gloves.

His fingers were doing the same sort of odd tingling, craving the touch of her.

How they managed to get through the dance, short as it wound up being, he would never know. They barely spoke another word throughout, letting their eyes, their hands, and their smiles converse for them, content, for the moment, with the prospect of after the dance to have much more.

Then, suddenly, he was bowing, and the room held applause for the dancers. Almost at once, Edward was moving toward Kitty, taking her hand and bringing it to his lips quickly, not caring if anyone would see or if he ever left that moment.

"Would it be terribly unbecoming to find a quiet moment alone now?" Kitty inquired softly, her voice tight, her gloved fingers flicking the underside of his chin.

Edward smiled, tilting his head curiously. "I don't think so, why?"

She sighed very briefly. "Because I think I'm dreaming, and I need to be sure that I'm not."

"And the way to do that is…?"

103

The blush that immediately flooded her cheeks triggered a tightening of his throat, and he endeavored to clear the blockage. "Right, now I'm the one dreaming, but I have no intention of waking up. Come on, I'll find us a place."

He tugged her from the dance floor, though she was hard on his heels, her free hand folding over their clasped ones. He had been to the Sterlings' home several times before, but it was suddenly impossible to think of a single place they could go. Out of the ballroom and into the corridor, looking this way and that for any alcove, any open space, any room…

"Here," he suddenly gasped, turning down a new corridor and stopping, facing Kitty at once.

She looked up at him, her smile somehow more stirring than any he had seen yet. "Is this where I tell you that I love you?" she asked him, raising a hand to his jaw.

He turned his face to kiss her palm, then reached out to stroke her cheek. "Only if you do, my love," he whispered, unable to believe any of this was happening.

"I do love you," she insisted, her voice hitching. She shook her head, her eyes welling. "I don't know how I missed it for so long."

Edward leaned in, kissing her brow. "You missed nothing. It would never be too late nor take too long. Never. I would have waited for eternity and only counted myself fortunate to ever be loved by you in the slightest."

Kitty's hand slid to his neck, another shaking inhale racking her. "I don't deserve to be loved by you. Not like this, not so much. I don't."

He nuzzled against her gently. "Yes, you do," he breathed, his lips dusting her cheek. "You deserve all the adoration in the world, to be treasured for eternity, to have everything. You hear me? Everything."

He pressed his lips to hers then, finding them soft, eager, and generous in her untutored fervor. There were no words for the feeling of them, for the pressure of her hand at his neck, for the way she arched closer to him in less than half a heartbeat. He wrapped his arms around her, cradling her against him and only feeling more awestruck with every passing brush of her lips. She trembled in his arms, and he was not entirely certain he did not tremble in hers.

Footsteps in the corridor beyond broke them apart, and, when they were certain they had not been spotted, Edward leaned down to capture her lips again, this time with brief insistence.

"Do you believe that we're awake now?" he asked her with a low chuckle.

Kitty grinned up at him, her fingers running up and down his neck in a delicious manner. "Do you?"

"No," Edward said simply. "And I don't know that I ever will." He kissed her once more, then sighed, taking her hand. "Shall we go and tell the others?"

Kitty nodded eagerly, her fingers lacing through his at once. "Yes! Everyone is here, even Charlotte. It is the perfect time."

This time, Edward let her lead, content to follow wherever she would go. "You should know something, my love," he murmured.

She glanced over her shoulder. "Should I?"

"I have a wager with Charlotte," he admitted with a wince. "About marriage. We made it some weeks ago. Whoever marries first gets a hundred pounds. And the loser has to name their first child after them. I only had you in mind, but I cannot apologize enough for the indignity."

Kitty's brows rose. "You wagered on me?"

"It wasn't like that," Edward assured her as they reentered the ballroom. "I was tired of being afraid of courting you, of trying for you, so I thought if I had this challenge with Charlotte—"

"I'm not upset," she interrupted, her thumb rubbing over his hand. "It's just…" She gave him a shy, adorable smile. "Were you that certain of me?"

Relieved and even more in love than a moment before, Edward shook his head. "No. But I was certain I had to try. There was no one else I could ever imagine feeling this for, no one else I wanted to try for. Just you."

Kitty grinned, her thumb now brushing his hand in a deeper pattern that burned the soles of his feet. "Then I'd say it was an excellent wager, wouldn't you? There's no one I want but you either. No one I can imagine."

"I love you," he whispered as his throat immediately grew

parched.

She winked at him, of all things. "And I you."

He squeezed her hand tightly, finally casting his eyes up to the group they were nearing.

"All we're missing is Hensh," he heard Charlotte bemoan with her usual dryness, her back to them as she addressed the rest of the group, "and I'll have a battalion."

Edward grinned. "You called?"

If it was possible to hear someone roll their eyes, he did so then. She turned to face them, her expression sour. "Oh, good," Charlotte grumbled. "I feel so much better now." She eyed their hands and raised a brow at Kitty. "Kitty Morton, have you come to tell us something to explain the glow in your cheeks?"

Kitty blushed, beaming still as her thumb continued to rub against Edward's. "Perhaps."

Izzy and Sebastian pushed forward, Izzy clasping her hands under her chin. "Well?"

Edward looked at Kitty, whose eyes were on him, smiling with the adoration and love they had so recently proclaimed. Kitty returned her attention to her brother and sister-in-law. "Lieutenant Henshaw has made me an offer of marriage, and I have accepted him."

"Thank God," Camden Vale said without any hesitation whatsoever. "Has anyone been waiting for this as long as I have?"

Several hands raised among the group. They had *all* known how he felt? And none of them had offered help or advice?

Edward glared at each of them in turn. "Marvelous help you all were here, thank you."

But none of that mattered anymore, he decided. Kitty loved him, and they would marry. Whether he won the wager with Charlotte or not, they would marry, and their future would be incomparable.

He didn't mind the name Charlotte anyway.

Not really.

Epilogue

What are endings but new beginnings? And was there such a terrifying notion in all the world as that? If nothing ever ends but only begins again, however do we stop the madness from continuing? This author cannot say, and there is an end. Pray, do not now begin again.

-The Spinster Chronicles, 13 August 1819

"You didn't plan for that, did you, Miranda?"

Miranda Sterling gave her sister a rather superior smile as she took in the adorable sight of Kitty Morton and her betrothed, Lieutenant Henshaw, sitting on a bench at this delightful garden party hosted by the Wrights. They were clearly in love, and their conversation was either the most fascinating one that ever existed, or their marriage would be taking place in very short order.

"Of course I did," Miranda answered with a laugh. "Anyone with eyes could see that Hensh was pining for the girl, but they were both so timid in that respect, someone needed a little push. There is nothing a bachelor loves so much as pursuing a girl someone else wants."

Arabella frowned a little. "But no one wanted Kitty; you said so yourself. The bachelors were not interested."

"But Hensh did not know that, did he?" Miranda laughed to herself, delighted still at the success of her little project. "As though I would have offered Kitty to any of those dear fellows I claimed to. None of them would have suited, though their prospects were fine enough. No, Hensh was the idea all along, and what a splendid match they will be!"

Sighing her usual sisterly long-suffering, Arabella shook her head. "And Charlotte Wright? What of her and that Mr. Sandford? You were rather keen on helping him win someone or other."

Miranda glanced over toward the Wrights' home, where Michael Sandford had just disappeared, and Charlotte Wright was now stomping toward. "Oh, I wouldn't worry about Michael and Charlotte. I daresay that will be settled in short order, as well."

"You are incorrigible," her sister grumbled, taking a long sip of lemonade. "I cannot believe we are related."

That was rich and utterly false. Arabella adored Miranda's mischief and was far more gossip hungry than she would ever admit to. There was no need to reply to such a falsehood, and Miranda only smiled at the adorable couple she might not have put together but had certainly hastened along.

Arabella sniffed softly. "All of your dear Spinsters will be married soon. What will your next enterprise be?"

Miranda chuckled to herself, knowing her sister's question was more a sign of her own interest rather than passing curiosity. "I have an option or two," she mused, tapping a finger against her glass.

"Which are?"

She shrugged a shoulder lightly. "*The Spinster Chronicles* will soon release their 'Best Bachelor' issue, and there is always such fervor about it. I might take an interest there."

"Or…?"

Miranda gave her sister a sidelong look, her grin slow. "I may venture out to Bristol. Lieutenant Henshaw has several sisters, and I've a fancy to put my hand to work in their favor."

Arabella groaned, shaking her head. "Oh, Miranda…"

"There's no hope for it, sister." Miranda giggled softly, loving each idea equally and wondering if she might pursue both. "I simply love intervening, and I am getting rather good at it. One never knows what fun could come from it all."

Coming Soon

We Don't Talk About Bachelors

The Bachelor Gazette

Book One

"Hell hath no fury like a
bachelor scorned..."

by

REBECCA CONNOLLY